P9-CMA-838

"So, you want to use me for great sex?" Ryan asked incredulously

"Would that be so bad?" Jessica asked, splashing him and playfully sticking out her tongue.

He chuckled. "Watch yourself, Jessie." His eyes grew darker as his gaze wandered over her wet body. "I can think of several ways to put that tongue of yours to good use...."

Jessica drew back slightly, seeming a little startled by his blatant desire.

Noticing her withdrawal, Ryan joined her in the tub. "Now, don't go getting modest on me again," he teased, giving her a devastatingly sexy grin. "I need you completely uninhibited by the time we make love."

"And just when do you think that will be?" she asked boldly, rubbing her bare shoulder against his chest.

He barely managed to resist the urge to kiss that sassy mouth of hers and take her, fast and furious, right there in the tub. Instead, he ran his finger down her cheek and said, "Don't worry, honey. You'll know..."

Dear Reader,

Seduced. The word alone conjures up all kinds of shameless possibilities, doesn't it? Sensual temptations, forbidden pleasures. You'll find all those and more between the pages of my latest BLAZE.

Ryan Matthews is a man who knows what he wants, and he's wanted sassy, sexy Jessica Newman in his bed for more than a year. Now he's going after her, and he'll do whatever it takes to make her his... including seducing her in the most delicious, sinful ways! His very innovative "cake scene" is sure to make you crave something sweet, and his inspiring "couples gift" will no doubt leave you breathless. Seduction has never been so hot!

I'd love to know what you think of *Seduced.* You can write to me at P.O. Box 1102, Rialto, CA 92377-1102, or at janelle@janelledenison.com. I always write back! For a list of upcoming releases, check out my Web site at www.janelledenison.com.

Fondly,

Janelle Denison

Books by Janelle Denison

HARLEQUIN TEMPTATION
679—PRIVATE PLEASURES
682—PRIVATE FANTASIES
732—FORBIDDEN
759—CHRISTMAS FANTASY
799—TEMPTED

Don't miss any of our special offers. Write to us at the following address for information on our newest releases.

Harlequin Reader Service
U.S.: 3010 Walden Ave., P.O. Box 1325, Buffalo, NY 14269
Canadian: P.O. Box 609, Fort Erie, Ont. L2A 5X3

SEDUCED
Janelle Denison

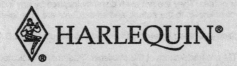

HARLEQUIN®

TORONTO • NEW YORK • LONDON
AMSTERDAM • PARIS • SYDNEY • HAMBURG
STOCKHOLM • ATHENS • TOKYO • MILAN • MADRID
PRAGUE • WARSAW • BUDAPEST • AUCKLAND

If you purchased this book without a cover you should be aware
that this book is stolen property. It was reported as "unsold and
destroyed" to the publisher, and neither the author nor the
publisher has received any payment for this "stripped book."

To all the readers who've written to let me know
how much they enjoy my stories. Thank you for
your kind words and friendship. This one's for you.

And to Don, whose support, encouragement and love
make each story a reality.

ISBN 0-373-25911-5

SEDUCED

Copyright © 2000 by Janelle Denison.

All rights reserved. Except for use in any review, the reproduction or
utilization of this work in whole or in part in any form by any electronic,
mechanical or other means, now known or hereafter invented, including
xerography, photocopying and recording, or in any information storage
or retrieval system, is forbidden without the written permission of the
publisher, Harlequin Enterprises Limited, 225 Duncan Mill Road,
Don Mills, Ontario, Canada M3B 3K9.

All characters in this book have no existence outside the imagination of
the author and have no relation whatsoever to anyone bearing the same
name or names. They are not even distantly inspired by any individual
known or unknown to the author, and all incidents are pure invention.

This edition published by arrangement with Harlequin Books S.A.

® and TM are trademarks of the publisher. Trademarks indicated with
® are registered in the United States Patent and Trademark Office, the
Canadian Trade Marks Office and in other countries.

Visit us at www.eHarlequin.com

Printed in U.S.A.

1

"MR. MATTHEWS, Jessica Newman is here to see you."

The voice of Haywood and Irwin's receptionist drifted through the intercom on Ryan Matthews' desk, breaking his train of thought on the brief he was preparing for a client's divorce case.

Before he could recover from Glenna's unexpected announcement, she continued in her ever-efficient manner. "Ms. Newman doesn't have an appointment, but said she'd like to speak with you regarding a personal matter if you have the time."

Curiosity flickered through Ryan, as well as an undeniable spark of enthusiasm. He'd make the time for Jessica Newman—anytime, anyplace. That she'd sought *him* out was enough to pique his interest, especially when she'd made it abundantly clear the last time he'd seen her that there could never be anything between them. Although he'd sensed a mutual attraction at the time, she'd diverted it with a collection of lawyer jokes he'd found too amusing to be offensive.

"My afternoon is clear, Glenna." He didn't have any appointments or engagements, just a tedious pile of correspondence awaiting his attention. No doubt, Jessica would provide a much more exciting diversion. "Will you show her to my office, please?"

The line disconnected, and Ryan set aside the documents he'd been reviewing and straightened the scattering of folders and papers on his desk, all the while wondering what had prompted this unscheduled visit of hers.

He'd first met Jessica a year ago when he and his buddies, Marc and Shane, had headed up to the Colorado Rocky Mountains for a few days of skiing. But instead of the guys-only weekend they'd envisioned, they'd found themselves sharing the same cabin with Jessica, her sister, Brooke, and another friend, Stacey. A blizzard had stranded Brooke and Marc together for two days in a deserted cabin, which had been the beginning of a lasting relationship between the two. And while Shane had also connected with Stacey on a very intimate level, Ryan had struck out with Jessica, but not for lack of trying.

Over the past twelve months he'd seen her a handful of times, the last of which had been at Marc and Brooke's small, intimate wedding three weeks ago where they'd stood up as best man and maid of honor for the couple. Other than Stacey and Shane, only immediate family had been invited to the private gathering.

And once again, Jessica had opposed his flirtatious advances. She'd used her arsenal of lawyer jokes to keep her attraction to him at bay, and ultimately turned down his request to take her out to dinner sometime. He'd been prepared for her refusal—over the course of a year she'd rejected him more than any man's ego should have to endure. More than most men *would have* endured.

He wasn't most men, and possessed enough patience to believe that some things were worth waiting for. And Jessica intrigued him with her efforts to resist him. She stimulated him with her sassy mouth and spirited debates. And it drove him nuts that he couldn't break through that reserve of hers and make her admit to the awareness simmering between them.

She'd become a challenge, one he enjoyed as much as it frustrated him—losing, in any capacity, wasn't something he liked to accept, and he'd never been one to admit defeat until he'd exhausted every effort available.

A slow smile curved his mouth. Maybe it was time he upped the ante with a more direct approach and *showed* her that their attraction could lead to a mutually satisfying relationship. He wasn't looking for anything deep, heavy, or serious that would interfere with the goals he'd spent the past six years trying to achieve. No way did he want to disappoint his parents, who'd scraped and saved to send him through college and law school and were so proud that their only son had chosen such a distinguished career. Eventually, he wanted to make junior partner. There was also the possibility of him heading up the family law department, and he was biding his time, winning cases, and making a name for himself that would go a long way in impressing the higher-ups when the time came for that particular advancement.

Being a bachelor suited Ryan just fine—it freed him to pursue his career goals single-mindedly, without the distraction of a serious relationship to waylay him, as he'd seen with other colleagues. But he wasn't opposed to spending time with a woman who aroused him on all levels, and Jessica Newman certainly did that.

But first, he needed her to admit she reacted the same way to him.

His mind turned over tantalizing ideas just as his office door opened and Glenna stepped aside to let Jes-

sica enter. Automatically, he stood, one of the many
gentlemanly gestures ingrained by his mother since he
was a toddler. Being the only son in a family with three
sisters, he'd learned early to treat women with utmost
respect. As a teenager, he'd grumbled about the unfair-
ness of having to cater to his sisters, but had grown to
appreciate being familiar with the formalities that
women seemed to admire and value.

Not that he was counting on his social graces to
make any difference with Jessica. No, it was going to
take something more tangible and candid to make an
impact on her. By the time she left his office, he
planned to shake her aloof composure and, he hoped,
put a fracture in her convictions to keep him at arm's
length, too.

She strolled into the room, her winter coat draped
over her arm with her leather gloves stuffed in the
front pocket. He started around his desk and across the
distance separating them, watching as her big blue
eyes registered his gradual approach. He smiled, taking in her teal-and-black, thigh-length sweater over
black leggings, which tucked into stylish boots. She always dressed conservatively, whether in jeans and
loose blouses, or slacks and long flowing skirts—nothing to draw attention to the slender curves and full
breasts merely hinted at beneath her choice of clothing.

Nothing sophisticated like the kind of worldly
women his profession drew, but it was her whole-
someness that fascinated him and appealed to him. She
wore little makeup to enhance the creamy perfection of
her skin, just enough to intensify the drown-in-them-
forever blue of her eyes. Her hair was a rich shade of
honey-blond, all chin length in a no-fuss style, and
parted on the side with wispy bangs touching her fore-

head. The strands were incredibly silky-looking, beckoning for him to slide his fingers through them as he'd envisioned doing a hundred times since knowing her.

Today, there would be no suppressing his urges. Today, he was going to discover just how warm and heavenly her hair felt wrapped around his fingers...and he planned to discover a whole lot more.

"Can I bring either of you refreshments?" Glenna asked.

"Would you like something from the coffee bar downstairs?" he suggested to Jessica. "An espresso? Mocha? Cappuccino?"

He fully expected her to say she wasn't staying long, but she surprised him with, "I'd love a mocha, thank you. I'm still chilled from the cold temperatures outside. Maybe that will help warm me up."

Ryan thought of more traditional and fun ways to generate heat. Long, slow kisses. The stroke of his hands across her bare skin. His naked body against hers. The possibilities were endless.

"A mocha it is," he said, glancing toward Glenna with their order. "And I'll take a cappuccino."

With a nod, the receptionist was gone, closing the door behind her.

"This is a pleasant surprise." Taking her coat and purse, he hung both next to his suit jacket on the brass hooks mounted on the wall just inside the room. "Dare I hope that you've reconsidered going out on a date and you're here to beg me for a second chance?"

A smile quirked the corner of her mouth, and she slanted him that sly look he was coming to know so well. He knew what was imminent, and anticipated her brand of humor.

"Hmm, let's see," she murmured speculatively, as if

giving his question serious consideration. "I'm trapped in a room with a tiger, a rattlesnake, and a lawyer. I have a gun with two bullets. What should I do?"

He lifted his brows, indicating he was ready for her punch line, even though he knew it wouldn't bode well for him. "I have no idea. What should you do?"

"Shoot the lawyer. *Twice*." She flashed him a quick grin.

He chuckled and shook his head, even as he wondered what had caused such a cynical attitude toward attorneys. "I take it that means no?"

"Ahh, a lawyer that catches on quick. Amazing." She moved away from him, to the wall holding his law degree and other various certificates, diplomas and credentials he'd acquired since college. He watched her examine each one, a tiny frown forming on her brow. Not sure what had caused the sudden mood change, he attempted to keep their banter light and flirtatious. "You'd better be careful, Jessie. I have to confess that those lawyer jokes of yours are starting to turn me on."

She glanced over her shoulder at him, a hint of laughter dancing in her eyes. "Maybe I need to work on my delivery."

His gaze perused her lazily, thoroughly. "From my vantage point, your delivery is *perfect*." He gained a bit of satisfaction at the temptation he witnessed in her eyes, the wanting. What he didn't care for was the struggle to curb her desires. "I think what we need to work on is your general opinion toward lawyers, and me."

She turned around and sighed, the sound rife with regret. "It's nothing personal, Ryan. I *do* like you."

"Just not that I'm a man who represents clients in a court of law."

"Yeah, something like that," she responded vaguely.

Pushing his hands into his trouser pockets, he slowly stepped toward her, watched as she subtly backed up to keep the same amount of distance between them. "Then maybe we should narrow it down to working on just you, and me...on a *personal* level."

She bumped into his cherrywood filing cabinet, glared at it for being in her way, then crossed her arms over her chest in a gesture he read as protective. "You don't give up, do you?"

"What can I say? Being a lawyer, I like to argue and prove people wrong. Especially when I know I'm right."

She rolled her eyes at his too-confident statement. "Well, this is one case you won't win, counselor."

He smiled lazily. "You don't think so?"

She shook her head, and that soft, enticing hair of hers swayed with the movement, teasing him, making the tips of his fingers tingle for direct contact. "I *know* so."

Very casually, as if it were a perfectly natural move, he braced his left hand against the edge of the filing cabinet, sealing off her one chance to slip around him. All amusement ceased, replaced by a shimmering heat. Her scent, an arousing combination of jasmine and innocence, curled around him, intoxicating and impossibly alluring.

Resisting the urge to bury his face against her neck and inhale deeply of the fragrance clinging to her skin, he tipped his head and said, "Give me a strong, valid reason why I *should* give up."

She swallowed, and the pulse at the base of her

throat fluttered. "Number one on my list of dating rules. No lawyers. *Especially* divorce attorneys. It goes against my ethics."

He'd heard it all before, in so many words, and he didn't bother asking why, knowing by that guarded look in her eyes that he wouldn't glean the answer he wanted, just a brush-off. But he knew her reasons went much deeper than something so superficial, and the analytical part of him couldn't help but want to discover all her secrets.

"So, you're gonna hold my profession against me?"

"'Fraid so." She lifted her chin. "You know, despite knowing how much you enjoy provoking me, I didn't come here for an interrogation."

He stared deep into her eyes, filled with conflicting emotions. Denial. Defiance. Longing. It was the last emotion that struck a reciprocating chord in him.

"Maybe you came here for more than you realize," he murmured, and lifted his free hand. He moved slow and easy, catering to her apprehension, intending to brush his knuckles across her cheek, gently tangle his fingers through her silken hair, stroke along the warm nape of her neck...and let desire take its natural course.

He was determined to make this the defining moment between them. And judging by the deepening of her breathing, the parting of her lips, and the way her lashes drooped slumberously over her hazy eyes, he was fairly certain she wouldn't belt him for satiating the need to caress her supple skin, taste her honeyed lips, and draw her lithe form up against his hard, hungry body.

It never happened.

A brisk knock on the door interrupted his seduction. Jessica jerked back, shaken, her eyes widening in alarm. Inches away from touching her, he fisted his fingers in the air, and swore beneath his breath at Glenna's untimely return.

Frustration tightened his jaw. Another five seconds, and he would have finally kissed Jessica, as deeply and as intimately as she would have allowed. And in the process he would have put a serious crimp in her "ethics" against getting involved with a lawyer. He'd waited a year for this opportunity, only to have his proficient receptionist shatter the moment.

He gave Jessica the breathing room she suddenly seemed to need and opened the door, retrieving their hot beverages from Glenna. Out of the corner of his eye he saw Jessica move into the center of the room, where it was spacious and safe. She dragged a hand through her hair, looking flustered and as though she couldn't believe what she'd almost allowed him to do, what she'd almost openly participated in.

He nearly laughed at her naivete. If she knew the half of what he imagined doing to her, he was convinced he'd never see her again. Kisses and stolen caresses were only the beginning of what he wanted from her.

He turned back to the receptionist, who was awaiting further instructions from him. "Glenna, will you hold all my calls until I'm through with Ms. Newman?" At her nod, he added with a rueful grin, "And would you mind closing the door for me since my hands are full?"

"Of course." With a smile that told him she believed this was just another business meeting with a client, she enclosed them in the room. A tension-filled silence immediately descended over his office.

Jessica eyed him cautiously, and he hated that her

wariness was back. "You don't have to hold your calls for me."

He held her cup out to her, and she took her beverage. "I prefer private, uninterrupted consultations."

A faint smile touched the corner of her mouth. "Are you going to charge me by the hour for your time?" She took a drink of her mocha, then her tongue darted out, catching the smear of whipped cream clinging to her upper lip.

His gut clenched, and he drew a deep, steady breath, unable to remember the last time a woman had him so tied up in knots. "For you, my fee is negotiable, and very flexible." He winked at her to put her at ease. "But we can discuss that later. Have a seat and let's get business out of the way first."

He waved to one of the two seats in front of his desk while he settled into his leather chair. He caught a glimpse of the gray-leaded sky out the floor-to-ceiling windows that dominated the Denver high-rise where Haywood and Irwin leased their offices, and wondered if they were in for another winter storm.

Taking a quick drink of his cappuccino, he set his cup on his blotter and reclined in his chair. "You have my complete and devoted attention, not to mention my curiosity. What brings you by my office in the middle of the day?"

"I wanted to discuss something with you." A sudden anxious light flickered in her gaze. "I suppose I should have called first, but I was the next block over having lunch with Brooke, so I thought I'd take a chance that you were in and available. I figured a half hour out of your afternoon might be easier and more convenient than taking time out of your evening."

He lifted a brow her way. Easier and more convenient for her, of course. "Don't be shocked, but my social calendar in the evenings is quite empty, though I wouldn't mind filling in a few of those nights with a date, or two, or three, with you."

She wrinkled her nose at him, and this time didn't bother responding to his flirtatious attempt to sway her. He chalked up another rejection, but wasn't the least bit discouraged.

She took another drink of her flavored coffee, then stated what was on her mind. "I want to do something special and fun for Brooke and Marc since they had such a small ceremony and no reception."

"From what I remember, they didn't want a reception," he interrupted, remembering his friend's request to keep their wedding small and simple, which had included no gifts from the guests.

"True. My sister felt that since this was her second marriage she'd keep things low key." Though Jessica's tone held mild reproach for her sibling's sensible characteristic, her affection for Brooke was unmistakable. "But I'd really like to throw a surprise reception party in their honor, to give family and friends the opportunity to congratulate them, too. And since you and I were best man and maid of honor at the wedding, I thought it would be appropriate if *we* hosted the party. I also thought New Year's Eve would be a romantic and fun evening to celebrate their marriage."

He glanced at the open engagement calendar on his desk for the month of December, noting that the new year was only four weeks away. "That sounds great, but aren't most halls and ballrooms already booked for New Year's Eve parties by now?"

"Well, this is where I need your help." Grinning impishly, she shifted in her seat, and crossed one slender leg over the other. "Brooke has mentioned in passing that your house is huge, and I was hoping that's where we could have the party. Obviously, we can't do it at my apartment, and yes, I did check into various halls and ballrooms and couldn't find any place that wasn't already reserved. You're my last hope."

He liked that she might have to depend on him for something, which meant he'd gain leverage to reap something in return...like her acquiescence for a date.

Unfortunately, he wasn't sure he could accommodate her request. "My house isn't *huge*." Granted, the twenty-five hundred square feet of living space he'd purchased a little over a year ago sometimes seemed monstrous and too damned quiet and lonely in the evenings. He had his cat, Camelot, to keep him company though, and she was the perfect roommate. Female and loving, she didn't make unrealistic demands on his time and never complained about his sometimes grueling work schedule and late nights.

Absently, Jessica tucked a swath of hair behind her ear, revealing a small diamond stud earring that sparkled with her slightest movement. Not surprisingly, Ryan found her lobe incredibly sexy, and wondered if he'd elicit a shiver or moan from her should he ever have the pleasure of nibbling on that soft, enticing piece of flesh.

"Can it accommodate about thirty people?" she asked, bringing his musings back to the present.

He rubbed his thumb along his jaw as he considered her question. "If they're spread out between the living room, dining room, and family room on the bottom level. And if we move my furniture around to make more open space."

"We can make it work." The exuberance brightening

her features made him realize how much this party meant to her, and just how close she was to her sister.

From the sketchy details Ryan had learned at Brooke's wedding, they had no other siblings. Their mother lived in West Virginia with her second husband, and when he'd casually asked Jessica about her father, he'd received a cool, emotionless response that their real father was no longer a part of their lives and hadn't been for some time. It was all the information he'd gleaned, but it had been enough for him to suspect that she'd had a rough childhood.

She set her nearly empty cup on the small table between the two chairs, her eyes brimming with excitement. "We'll send Brooke and Marc a separate invitation on the pretense of you having a New Year's Eve celebration so they'll be surprised and won't try and talk us out of the party."

He took a drink of his warm cappuccino and didn't reply to her monologue, since she wasn't really asking for his input. He hadn't said yes to using his house, either, but Jessica was obviously way ahead of him on that score and assuming that he'd agree. She had the party all planned out in her mind, and he was getting the distinct impression that he was just along for the ride.

He intended to veer her off course and make the excursion much more interesting.

"I'll take care of the other invitations, the decorations, catering, and a cake, and if you have a stereo system I'll bring along some CDs with romantic music that we can play." She grinned, bowling him over with that guileless smile that lacked her normal sass or reserve. "And I'll find a gift that I know they'll both enjoy, which we can go in on together, if you'd like. You won't have to worry about a thing except writing up a speech to toast the newlyweds."

How convenient, he thought in amusement, knowing exactly what she was attempting to do—take complete charge and keep his interaction with her to a minimum. "And splitting the cost of the party with you, of course."

"I'll keep the expenses as minimal as possible. I promise. And if the expense of the party gets to be too much for you, I'll cover the costs."

Money wasn't a concern for him. Not in the least. "I can afford whatever you have in mind."

She leaned forward in her chair expectantly, her eyes hopeful. "Then the party is a go at your place?"

He saw this idea of hers as his last opportunity to insinuate himself in her life, to work past those barriers she put up with him, to spend quality time with her and tempt and seduce her, and see where their attraction might lead.

Picking up his favorite Mont Blanc pen, he rolled it between his fingers. "I'll agree to the party at my place on one condition."

She made a snickering sound. "You can't agree without striking some kind of bargain, can you?"

"I can't help it." He shrugged. "Making deals is part of my business. Why settle for less than what I know I can get?"

"Call it what it is, Matthews—wearing your opponent down."

He feigned a wince at her barb. "I'd like to think of it as drive and ambition to succeed. I haven't gotten as far as I have without it."

Derision colored her gaze. "In your illustrious career as a divorce attorney, or with me?"

Somewhere along the way their conversation had taken a personal slant, and it seemed as though his ambitious nature was a source of contention for her. "With both, actually."

The leg crossed over her opposite knee bounced impatiently. "All right then, counselor, let's hear it. What are your conditions?"

He set his pen in its holder. "That I'm part of the planning, every step of the way."

Her jaw dropped, and she stared at him incredulously. "You're joking."

He blinked, and kept his face carefully blank. "I'm completely serious."

"You don't have time to do the planning," she insisted, obviously rattled by his suggestion and what it implied—spending time with him.

"How do you know what I have time for?"

She shook her head in an attempt to divert his interest. "I work out of my apartment with my medical transcripts, and can take care of calls and errands during the day. Why would you want to worry about any of this when I'm more than willing to handle everything?"

Knowing if he revealed his true motives he'd never stand a chance with her, he opted for the obvious. "Well, for starters, I'm paying for half of this party, which gives me the right to contribute my opinion on everything, yes?"

Very reluctantly, she said, "Well...yes."

"And I'm opening my house to thirty-something people, so I'd like to know what to expect, and what you plan to do." He flipped through his daily calendar and summed up his schedule fairly quickly. "I do have some court appearances coming up and cases that I need to close, but for the most part my nights and weekends are wide open."

Frustration all but radiated from her—there was nothing she could refute. She sat back in her chair with a small huff. "Why don't sharks attack lawyers?"

Suppressing a grin, he reached for a piece of letterhead and retrieved his pen again. "Why?"

"Professional courtesy," she muttered.

He chuckled deeply as he drew a diagram to his house for her. "Is that your way of saying I got my way?"

"Yeah, you got your way." She didn't sound happy about the fact.

He added his address and home phone number to the piece of paper. Standing, he circled around the desk and handed her the stationery with his bold script on it. "Here are directions to my place. How about we start on the planning tomorrow since it's Saturday? I'm free—how about you?"

Tentatively, she took the heavy cream vellum from his outstretched hand, but didn't bother looking at it. "Unfortunately, I don't have any plans, either."

"Great. Why don't you come over around eleven and take a look at the layout of my house and see what we have to work with, and then we'll go from there?"

"All right." She folded the paper into a precise square. "I have a list of Marc and Brooke's close friends, and I have a program on my computer that can print up nice party invitations, so I'll do that this evening, get them addressed, and drop them in the mail on my way to your place in the morning."

He leaned his backside against the edge of his desk and crossed his legs at his ankles. "Bring them over and we'll address them together."

Her lips pursed. "I can do it myself. It's really a one-person job."

"Regardless, I want to be a part of every aspect of this party, Jessie." He knew if he gave her an inch, she'd run a mile. "Including addressing and stamping the invitations."

Her chin lifted a stubborn notch. "It's *Jessica.*"

"I like Jessie better." The nickname was soft, gentle, with just a hint of rebellion. "It suits you."

She clucked her tongue. "I suppose you could call me worse."

He dropped his voice to a low, husky murmur for effect. "Like honey, or sweetheart?"

Her cheeks flushed a sudden, telltale pink. "Those endearments *definitely* don't apply to me and you." Finishing the last of her mocha, she stood and pitched the empty cup into the wastebasket at the side of his desk.

"They could." He twisted around to keep her in his line of vision as a sudden thought dawned on him. "Unless you're dating someone else?"

"No," she admitted freely. "I'm single, available, but not interested...in you."

Then it was up to him to change her mind, because her lying words contradicted the wistful look in her gaze.

She broke eye contact first. "Well, I think we just about covered everything, and now that you've blackmailed me, I think I'll be on my way." She headed toward the door, and he followed right behind.

"Just one more thing," he said with a lazy, self-assured smile.

Her gaze narrowed skeptically as she reached for her coat. "What? Another condition?"

He gently grabbed her wrist before she could execute her move, startling her. Instantaneous awareness cloaked them. She sucked in a swift breath, but didn't struggle or pull back. Their gazes locked as he stroked his thumb over the pulse point at the base of her wrist. In gradual degrees, he eased closer to her, while she stood statue-still.

He watched as her irises turned as dark and sensual as crushed sapphire velvet, and a surge of heat sped through his veins. Their thighs brushed, and he heard her breath hitch in her throat. Unwilling to let this moment pass without indulging in one of his tamer fantasies, he lifted his hand and finally skimmed his fingers along her smooth cheek, savoring the suppleness of her skin.

She looked stunned by his boldness, mesmerized by the tenderness of his touch. Taking advantage of her uncharacteristic docility, he gave in to the impulse he'd been denied earlier and slid his fingers into her hair. Silky warmth engulfed him, like nothing he'd ever experienced. The sensation was so unbelievably erotic he shuddered with pleasure.

"Ryan?" she whispered, her voice holding a slight tremor.

"No more conditions," he said, his tone low and rough. Fisting his hand into the feathery mass, he tipped her face up, so she could look into his eyes and see his intent. "This has nothing to do with the party, and everything to do with you and me...and finally getting an answer to a question I've been wanting to ask for the past year."

And then he lowered his head and settled his mouth over hers.

2

JESSICA NEVER COULD HAVE anticipated the impact of Ryan's kiss, or her open response to him. A year's worth of resisting his charm, teasing and advances dissolved the moment his mouth touched hers, unraveling every solid lecture she'd given herself on why she could never fall for a man like him...a man who made a career out of tearing families apart, just as her family had been ripped apart.

But none of that mattered at that moment, not when the man, not the lawyer, was gently coaxing her with the soft glide of his lips across hers, taking time and care to draw her into far more forbidden territory. She had no defense against his brand of lazy seduction, his hypnotic patience. And when he slid his other hand into her hair, gradually eased her back against the wall and slanted her mouth more firmly beneath his, she was totally and completely lost. She gripped his corded forearms for support, bared by his rolled-up shirtsleeves, and held on.

Aching to experience more of this exquisite pleasure, she surrendered with a breathy moan. Her lips softened and parted beneath his, and his tongue swept inside to taste her, tantalizing her with silken, gliding forays that made her knees weak and her head spin. She brazenly sought a more intimate sampling, too, and shivered at the combined flavors of hot male and rich coffee.

She learned quickly that despite his straightforward manner, he was a man who took his time and did things thoroughly. He kissed her with delicious languor, as if he had all the time in the world to indulge in the taste and textures of her mouth. His hips pressed closer, making her all too aware of the unyielding masculine body pinning her to the wall, the citrus scent of his aftershave, and the voluptuous sensations coursing through her.

His thumbs brushed her jaw, and her skin caught fire. His wide chest grazed hers, and her breasts swelled and her nipples tightened and ached. A muscular thigh insinuated itself between hers, she felt the hard length of his erection against her hip, and heated desire curled low in her belly. And when he deepened the kiss, she responded just as enthusiastically.

She'd never experienced passion like this—instantaneous and wild. Never wanted another man with such shameless abandon. Never allowed herself to be so reckless with her desires. Her one and only quick, awkward encounter with someone she'd briefly dated three years ago hadn't prepared her for such intense, thrilling pleasure and consuming need.

Ever since her sister's marriage she'd been feeling restless, wanting something that felt just beyond her reach. With a kiss, Ryan tapped into deeper longings, and made her crave *more*.

While her body wanted to see where all this irresistible ecstasy might lead, her sensible mind reminded her that any kind of relationship with him was impossible. Having witnessed the pain of her mother's separation, along with experiencing the anguish of abandonment, she'd learned to be cautious and selective when it came to men in general. By Ryan's own admission, his ambition to succeed was his main focus, and wouldn't leave much spare room in his life to cultivate a commitment to something other than his career. She'd spent the past year dodging his flirtatious overtures, turning him down, swearing never to court the kind of disaster imminent with a driven man like him, whose profession contradicted everything she believed in and wanted for herself...love, marriage and family.

A kiss, no matter how exciting and earth-shattering, wouldn't change her mind or her principles...or allow her to overlook the fact that he terminated families and marriages without thought to the injured parties involved in those cases.

As if sensing her sudden doubts, he slowly dragged his soft, damp lips from hers. His hot, ragged breath along her cheek added to the arousing sensations, and she bit her bottom lip to keep from releasing his name on a breathless, plaintive sigh.

"In case you're wondering, the answer was yes," he murmured huskily in her ear, then lifted his head and gently untangled his fingers from her hair.

Trying to regain her own equilibrium, she braced the flat of her palms against the wall behind her and forced her lashes open to look at him. Though his body no longer touched hers, he only stood a few inches away, and she could still feel the sizzling heat radiating from him. His eyes were heavy-lidded and dark, his irises a rich shade of brown rimmed in a glittering gold. Hungry eyes. Seductive eyes. His thick, sable hair was tousled around his head enticingly, and he looked very sexy and overwhelmingly male.

"What was the question?" she asked, her mind foggy and confused.

A crooked, full-of-himself smile curved his lips. "Do you want me as much as I want you?"

She'd forgotten all about his original quest to achieve an answer to his personal query. What she desperately needed was a lawyer joke to diffuse the too-intimate moment, but he had her so unbalanced she couldn't remember the simplest of her attorney witticisms.

Frowning, and without thinking, she touched her bottom lip, which was still moist, swollen and incredibly sensitive. "And you think I said yes with that kiss?"

"You most definitely didn't say no, and I always look for the positive." He slipped his hands into the front pockets of his olive-colored trousers. "Now that we have that awkward question out of the way, we can move on to the next logical phase of our attraction."

She laughed at his presumptuousness, but couldn't deny just how adorable he looked, and just how much he *did* appeal to her, physically and intellectually. He sparked something utterly shameless within her, made her want to throw caution to the wind and give in to that attraction he spoke of.

"And what do you consider the next logical phase?" she asked.

"A date."

Nothing she hadn't already heard and turned down before. She inclined her head and smiled. "Don't you think you're going about things backwards? A kiss first, date second?" Deeming it way past time she left, she reached for her coat.

He beat her to it, and held open the wool garment for her. "I've never been accused of being traditional."

She wasn't surprised. How could a man whose main objective was to split up married couples believe in romantic customs and idealistic sentiments?

She slipped into her coat with a murmured thanks, and turned around. His hands lingered, adjusting the collar, his thumbs grazing her neck. Of course her traitorous body shivered at that delectable caress, and her mind conjured up images of him gliding those long tapered fingers elsewhere.

He handed her purse to her, and she slung the long leather strap over her shoulder. "What if I'm a traditional kind of girl?"

An appropriately contrite look transformed his gorgeous features, though his eyes danced with a teasing light. "Then I apologize profusely for offending your delicate sensibilities with that kiss, and would like to make up for my atrocious behavior with dinner. How about tomorrow night?" He opened the door to his office and waited for her to precede him.

She stepped out into the hall, and realized he intended to escort her out—and felt ridiculously pleased by the gesture. "I'll be seeing you tomorrow morning, and we'll be spending the afternoon together."

"That's business. I'm referring to pleasure."

The word "pleasure" rolled off his tongue like a silken, seductive stroke along her spine. She drew a breath and resisted its allure. "No."

"Sunday night, then?"

He lightly rested his hand on the base of her back. Her coat was heavy and lined, yet that subtle pressure was enough to incite her feminine nerves and send a feverish awareness swirling within her. She held on to her standards and her respectability with both hands. "No."

"Okay," he said, unperturbed by her steadfast refusal. "You name the night, then."

His unwavering persistence amazed her. "How about never?"

They passed through the receptionist area, Ryan told Glenna that he'd be right back after escorting her to the lobby, and they continued to the alcove holding the bank of elevators.

He punched the down arrow and met her gaze. "You're going to make me work for this, aren't you?" He didn't seem at all bothered by that notion. In fact, Jessica suspected the challenge appealed to him and his lawyer instincts.

With his good looks and easy-going charm, she was certain he'd never had to work for a date in his life, and was ninety-nine percent sure his interest in her would wane once she capitulated to his relentless pursuit. No matter how easy it would be to surrender to Ryan despite his profession, it could never happen. She didn't intend to end up hurt and discarded by any man once he decided the fun was over—especially by one who affected her so strongly and threatened her emotions so severely.

The elevator pinged, signaling its arrival, and they both stepped into the lift. She pressed the button for the lobby, and waited until the metal doors closed. Her stomach dipped, from the descent of the elevator, or from being trapped in such a tiny cubicle with Ryan, she wasn't sure.

"I'm doing both of us a big favor," she finally said, infusing her voice with a suitable amount of regret that felt overwhelmingly real. "It would be ridiculous after that kiss to deny that I'm attracted to you, but I don't think we're looking for the same things in a relationship."

He flashed her a quick, tempting grin. "Chemistry is a great start."

They definitely had plenty of that, but she wanted something more permanent with a man, something more enduring and emotional. Stability and security—the very things she'd grown up without. "Which rarely lasts once the relationship turns physical."

He studied her too intently with those deep brown eyes of his. "Is that your experience?"

She shrugged vaguely and broke eye contact, unwilling to admit that her experience was limited, and did not evoke pleasant memories. "What's the longest relationship you've ever had?" she asked, turning the conversation back to him.

He worked his mouth in thought. "A little over a year."

Retrieving her lined leather gloves from her coat pocket, she pulled them on. "How long ago?"

"My senior year in high school."

She rolled her eyes at him, not at all surprised to discover that he'd spent most of his adult life avoiding a commitment with a woman, which was pretty much equivalent to him confirming himself as a bachelor. "You just proved my point about you and lasting relationships. They don't exist for you."

"You didn't prove anything," he refuted calmly. "After high school, I went to college while holding down a part-time job, then went straight into law school. Becoming a lawyer and establishing myself has taken precedence over a relationship."

"And your career is your number one priority." And

that kind of focus didn't leave much time to nurture an intimate relationship.

Not that she cared.

"I haven't gotten as far as I have without working hard and making sacrifices." His words weren't at all defensive, just a statement of fact. "And quite honestly, I haven't met a woman who's made me want to give up being a bachelor."

The velvet timbre of his voice, the flicker of something far more promising in his eyes, shot a distinct and unnerving tingle through her. The elevator came to a whirring stop, and she opened her purse and dug through the contents, using the search for her car keys as a much needed visual diversion. "I doubt I'm that woman, Matthews, and you're definitely not someone I'd consider anything long-term with, either."

"Something short-term then?"

Unable to tell if he was serious or joking, she slanted him a quick glance. The sinful invitation in his gaze indicated his suggestion was, indeed, an earnest one. Temptation crooked its finger, and it took more than a little effort to abstain from accepting his beguiling proposal.

None too soon, the door whooshed opened, and she stepped into the marbled lobby. "You're a rogue, and I'm not interested."

"You're not a very good liar, Jessie," he said in that silky tone of his. "You're definitely interested."

He stopped in the middle of the lobby, and she continued on to the main entrance. Then he called out after her. "And just for the record, I plan to wear down that resolve of yours."

She turned and used her backside to push open the glass doors that enclosed the interior of the building.

Her breath caught, at the afternoon chill that swirled around her, and at the vision of Ryan leaning against a tiled column, so utterly confident, so inherently sexual, so completely irresistible.

But resist him she would. She flaunted a grin full of fabricated sass. "You can certainly try, counselor, but don't expect me to make it easy on you. And don't expect to win."

He tipped his head, and a lock of dark hair fell across his brow, adding to his appeal. "You making it easy on me wouldn't be any fun, now would it?" he drawled. The devastatingly wicked grin claiming his lips told her he accepted her dare and anticipated the challenge. "See you tomorrow morning."

RYAN PUSHED HIMSELF to swim an additional ten laps on top of the fifteen he'd already accomplished, hoping the extra morning exercise would burn off the restless energy that had kept him tossing and turning for most of the night. Also to blame were the vivid fantasies that had invaded what little sleep he'd been able to snatch. Of Jessica beautifully naked and submissive in his bed. Of him discovering those curves she'd hidden beneath her bulky sweater, skimming his hands along quivering flesh, tasting her with his tongue, making her want him to the point of begging him for release.

And she begged so prettily in his fantasy, so sweetly. But before he could experience the ecstasy of burying himself deep inside her softness and warmth, he awoke from the erotic dream with a start. He'd been hard and aching, the sheets tangled around his bare legs, and sweating despite the cool night air washing over his body. Three times she'd brought him to the edge last night, until he'd finally dragged himself from bed at dawn and put himself through a rigorous work-out regimen in hopes of diminishing the lust that gripped him.

The sharpness of desire had ebbed, but he still wanted her.

Reaching the deep end of the pool, he executed a flip, accelerated off the wall, and continued his fluid, precise strokes across the surface. Curls of steam rose from the water he kept heated in the winter so he could use the pool on a daily basis, but his lungs burned from drawing in cold morning air. The muscles across his shoulders and down his back tingled from the exertion, while the warm water sluiced along his skin, his belly, his thighs, like a lover's caress.

Jessica's caress. And just like that, she'd joined him in the pool where he thought he was safe from those erotic fantasies with her.

The kiss they'd shared yesterday afternoon had ignited a dark, carnal craving he couldn't seem to shake, along with a deeper hunger that transcended mere sexual need, and emotions no other woman had ever evoked. For a year he'd let their desire for one another simmer, and now that he knew there was a warm and willing woman beneath that composed exterior, he wanted to discover everything about her, every sensual secret she harbored.

No easy feat, considering her maddening attempts to deny him, and her frustrating aversion to his profession. But that kiss had provided him with irrefutable evidence. Her vocal cords might be saying "no", but her lips had told him all he needed to know.

She wanted him, too.

Pulling himself out of the pool, he shivered as too-cold temperatures replaced the warmth of the water.

Grabbing the large, fluffy towel he'd left on a lounge chair, he dragged it over his wet head to remove the excess water from his hair, then wrapped the terry around his shoulders. He headed up the brick inlaid steps leading to his two-story house, and wasn't surprised to see his younger sister, Natalie, sitting at the small table in the kitchen nook that overlooked the landscaped backyard. As always, she'd made herself right at home and was reading his newspaper and drinking what he assumed was a mug of the coffee he'd made that morning. She saw him coming up the walkway, smiled gregariously, and waved.

He lifted a hand in greeting, but entered the house by way of a back door that led to one of the downstairs bathrooms, where he took a quick shower, washed his hair, and changed into the sweatshirt and jeans he'd left there earlier. Leaving his hair damp and finger-combed away from his face, he grabbed his socks and sneakers and headed into the kitchen to see his sister.

The unmistakable fragrance of the delicious buttermilk spice muffins his mother made assailed his senses. There was a cloth-lined basket on the table, and judging by the half-eaten muffin on the plate next to his sister, he'd identified the scent accurately.

"Morning, Nat." Taking one of the chairs across from her, he began pulling on his socks. "I'm glad to see that the house key I gave you for emergencies is coming in handy."

Unaffected by his wry tone, she set aside the paper he'd read earlier and shrugged. "I knocked, and no one answered. I didn't expect you to be out in the pool, for God's sake." She eyed him dubiously as she petted the fluffy gray ball of fur reclining on her lap. "How you can go swimming in fifty-degree weather and enjoy it is beyond me."

The pool was one of the things that had appealed to him when he'd bought the house, along with the large whirlpool in his master bath. "I keep the water heated, and it's invigorating."

"Whatever rocks your boat." Green eyes twinkling, she lifted her mug in a toast to him, then took a drink of the coffee.

Finished tying his shoes, he glanced at the clock, noted that he only had a half hour until Jessica arrived, and realized he needed to move his sister along her way. Unfortunately, Natalie was one to do things at her own unhurried pace.

At twenty-seven, she was the baby of the Matthews clan, and five years younger than he. Though he was close to all his sisters, he was especially fond of Natalie, whom he'd formed a special attachment to from the day his mother had brought her home from the hospital and he'd first peered into her bassinet. They were also the only two siblings left who were single and unattached.

"So, what brings you by?" he asked, wanting to get to the crux of her visit—if there was even a reason.

She glanced down at the cat she'd given him six months ago as a gift, so he'd have company in his big house. "I just wanted to make sure that Camelot isn't wanting for anything, isn't that right, Cammie?" she crooned, scratching the feline under her chin.

He couldn't help but grin at her excuse. "And?"

She tipped her head up, and her rich brown hair, permed with soft waves, swirled around her shoulders. "I found her lapping at a bowl of cream, and judging by her very affectionate purrs, I think she adores her master."

The cat was truly an affectionate pet, very spoiled, and he was just as smitten. "Now that you know Camelot has me wrapped around her paw, what *really* brings you by?"

She tore a hunk off the crispy top of the baked good, sprinkled with cinnamon sugared walnuts. "Mom wanted me to deliver something to you, along with these delicious muffins she made." She popped the bite into her mouth and chewed.

"Which you've helped yourself to, I can see." Unable to resist, he took a chunk of her muffin for himself. It all but melted in his mouth.

She licked the sugar from her fingers. "Of course," she replied unrepentantly. "It's not as though you have anyone else to share the muffins with."

He lifted a brow at her direct comment, but didn't feed the curiosity glimmering in her eyes. "You mind getting to the *real* reason why you're here?"

"I'll give you a hint. "You need to start practicing your 'ho, ho, hos' for Christmas Eve."

Remembering what had transpired last Christmas Eve, he guessed right away. "You brought the Santa suit over?"

"Yep. Mom wanted to make sure you had it beforehand. Christmas is only three weeks away, and I heard Jackie, Jennifer and Alyssa talking about Santa stopping over at Grandma's again this year. Looks like you started a new tradition."

He smiled at the mention of his nieces, whom he adored, the three of which belonged to his oldest sister, Courtney, and her husband Dale. He also had two nephews by his other sister, Lindsay, and her husband

Clive. The kids ranged in age from two to seven, and all still believed in the magic of St. Nick.

"I'd be happy to play Santa Claus." He glanced at the clock again, this time more meaningfully. "I hate to rush you off, Nat, but I've got company coming over." He ate the last of her muffin, then stood and started clearing off the table.

Natalie remained seated and continued stroking Camelot, watching as he tossed the newspaper into the trash, and took her mug and plate to the sink. "Hmm, if you're cleaning, your company must be female."

He slanted her a tolerant look. "Yes, she is."

Interest glimmered in her eyes. "Is it serious?"

If Jessica had her way, they'd remain platonic friends. If he had his way, she'd be warming his bed and fulfilling those fantasies that had him tied up in knots. But no matter how much he desired her, he wasn't about to rush her into something she wasn't emotionally prepared for. When the time was right, they'd make love. He'd waited a year for her to come around, so he could abstain a while longer, until he swayed her to his way of thinking. But until then, he planned to keep her just as aroused and inflamed as he was with touches and kisses and anything else she'd allow.

He wasn't sure how to answer his sister's question, so he kept his reply ambiguous. "I definitely like her."

"What's her name?"

"Jessica Newman." Rinsing the dirty plate and utensils in the sink, he placed them in the dishwasher. "She and I are planning a surprise party for Brooke and Marc on New Year's Eve, and she'll be here *anytime*."

She ignored his blatant hint to leave. "Are you going

to bring her over to Mom and Dad's for Christmas Eve?"

Drying his hands on a dish towel, he thought of that possibility. Christmas Eve at his parents' was a fun, cheerful, overnight affair, with baking, a buffet of food to snack on, and his mother playing Christmas music on the baby grand piano his father had bought her years ago for an anniversary present. There was laughter and reminiscing, and before the stroke of midnight they'd all retire to the rooms that they'd grown up in and wake up the next morning to enjoy the delight of watching the younger generation tear through the presents Santa had left for them.

He thought of Jessica, possibly spending the better part of Christmas alone, with her mother living in West Virginia, and Brooke now remarried. Would she accept such a personal invitation when she turned down the simplest of dates?

He'd never taken a woman to the family gathering before, never had the desire or the inclination to share that special time with someone else. Although it wasn't difficult to imagine Jessica fitting in with his family, he wasn't certain if *he* was ready for that leap and what it implied.

"I don't know if I'll ask her," he replied, as honest an answer as he'd give.

The doorbell rang, and Natalie's expression brightened with curiosity. Gently, she pushed Camelot to the floor, then stood, brushing the cat hairs from her black jeans. "Since your lady friend is here, I guess I should go."

"How convenient," he said drolly, knowing this was exactly what his sister had been stalling for. "Let me walk you to the door and introduce you."

STANDING ON RYAN'S front porch at eleven o'clock to the minute, Jessica drew a deep fortifying breath and adjusted the strap of her tote bag over her shoulder. The canvas bag held the notepad on which she'd started to plan Brooke and Marc's New Year's Eve party, along with the invitations and labels she'd printed up last night.

With luck, and the feminine strategy she had in mind, she'd be here an hour, max. Once she droned on about the tedious, boring party plans that would have most men fidgeting and thinking about the football game on TV, she was certain he'd change his mind about helping and be grateful that she'd handle all the details on her own. From there, any decisions she needed from him could be taken care of over the phone, and she wouldn't have to see him again until New Year's Eve.

And that suited her perfectly, she told herself with a decisive nod. The less direct involvement she had with sexy Ryan Matthews, Esquire, the better. No matter how much he tempted her, no matter that a single kiss from him had the ability to arouse her to the point of making her feel reckless and wild, absolutely nothing could come of their attraction. So why put herself through the added torment of spending so much unnecessary one-on-one time with Ryan?

Her determination melted the moment he opened the door and stood there, filling her senses with the seductive, drugging hunger she'd managed to squash since leaving his office yesterday afternoon. The tantalizing awareness returned with a vengeance, contradicting the lecture she'd just given herself.

Gone was the professional lawyer attire. With seemingly little effort, dressed in casual jeans and a sweatshirt, he still managed to look gorgeous and exude way too much confidence. It was December cold outside, but the heat in his dark eyes set her body on fire. The sensual promise of his smile made her want to toss her better judgment to the wind and experience all that had gone unexplored in her previous sexual encounter.

No doubt, Ryan would be happy to accommodate her, and satisfy her every whim. The thought sent a strange thrill racing through her, and had her mind tumbling with shameless possibilities.

"Amazing, a woman who's right on time," he said teasingly, and motioned her into the foyer with a sweep of his hand. "Come on in."

Shaking off the impossible thoughts stealing through her mind, she stepped inside the warmth of his house and opened her mouth to issue a lawyer joke in response to his male cynicism. The flow of words stopped when she saw another woman standing just inside the entryway, shrugging into a coat with a fur-lined collar.

The pretty and petite woman smiled. "Hi, Jessica, I'm Ryan's sister, Natalie," she introduced herself. "And I believe that wisecrack of my brother's comes from his scarred childhood and having to wait on his three sisters for the better part of his life."

Ryan sent a mock scowl Natalie's way, but there was affection in his gaze. "You have no idea what it's like to have to get up at four in the morning in order to take a shower for school before the three of you woke up and commandeered the bathroom. I was done in ten minutes, then had to sit around for three hours for the bus to arrive while the three of you fought for mirror space." He turned back to Jessica, and continued his argument. "And no matter how much time they all had to get ready, they were *never* on time for anything. Lindsay and Courtney were even late to their own weddings."

Deeming it her duty to stick up for her gender, Jessica added, "Obviously, their husbands think they were worth waiting for."

Her reply earned her a brilliant smile from Ryan's sister. "Oh, I do like you."

Ryan groaned. "Weren't you just leaving, Nat?"

"I'm gone." Natalie pressed a quick kiss to his cheek, then grasped Jessica's hand in hers. "It was nice meeting you. I hope we have the chance to get to know one another better."

Jessica didn't bother to correct the woman's assumption that she was Ryan's girlfriend. "It was nice meeting you, too."

Ryan blew out a breath once he closed the door behind his sister. "Ya gotta love her," he said with amusement, and helped her out of her jacket. "Especially since my parents keep insisting that she wasn't adopted."

Despite his joke, it was obvious that he loved his entire family very much. It wasn't what she'd expected. A part of her had assumed that his career choice had been based on his own personal family history being less than stable. Now, she wasn't so sure, which made her wonder what had inspired his choice of career.

She swallowed the personal question and retrieved her notepad from her bag. "I brought the invitations, and I thought I could draw out a diagram of the bottom level of your house so that I...I mean, *we* can figure out what we need to accommodate the guests."

"Let's get started," he said, too eagerly, too helpfully. "You can make notes while I give you the grand tour."

The "grand tour" left Jessica breathless. His house *was* huge in her estimation, when all she'd known was the one small home her family had lived in before her parents divorced, then the cramped space of apartments. Being self-employed and making a decent living as a medical transcriber, she'd upgraded to a nice complex in a middle-class neighborhood which she'd shared with Brooke until recently, but it didn't come close to the luxury in which Ryan lived.

Obviously decorated by a professional, in masculine colors of royal blue, hunter green, and chocolate brown, the lower level was spacious and spread out, affording them enough room to set up rental chairs for the party. The formal table in the dining room would hold the buffet she had in mind, and if they rearranged the furniture in the living room and family room they could add more seats there, too. The kitchen was a caterer's dream, with a huge wooden center island for them to use to prepare the appetizers.

As she gazed up the spiral staircase to the upper level, she imagined entwining evergreen and twinkling lights along the handrail and throughout the house to make it more enchanting. Cinnamon-scented candles would add to the ambiance. Flipping the page of her pad of paper, she made a notation under "florist" for poinsettias, holly and greenery, along with a few table arrangements.

"Did you want to see upstairs, too?" he asked once they'd covered the first level of the house.

She lifted her gaze from her notes and quirked her brow at him, feeling a tad suspicious. Up until this moment, he'd been very well behaved. "Is there anything up there I *need* to see?"

"The master bedroom?"

She bit the inside of her cheek to keep from grinning at the hopeful note in his voice, the inviting light in his gaze. "You plan on letting your guests mingle in there?"

A warm, private smile brushed across his mouth. "I'm only extending the invitation to you."

"It would be incredibly rude of us to leave our guests downstairs while we *mingle* upstairs," she said, deliberately misconstruing his meaning.

He followed her through the living room to the kitchen. "I'm sure our guests wouldn't miss us for an hour."

A delicious pressure tightened in her belly at his insinuation. An hour of pure ecstasy compared to the ten minutes of groping and fumbling she'd experienced three years ago.

Oh, wow.

Trying not to allow his sexy overture to entice her, she sat at the small kitchen table and withdrew the invitations, address labels and stamps. It was time to execute her scheme to discourage his interest in the party planning.

He didn't complain when she gave him the unpleasant job of licking the envelopes, and assigned him the monotonous task of affixing the return labels and stamps. Too cheerfully, he did as she instructed, not once shifting anxiously in his chair, or issuing an exasperated sigh.

Her ploy wasn't working. The man was impossible to dissuade. Not to mention that he had her completely distracted and unable to concentrate.

He was sitting so close, his leg occasionally grazed hers, the friction of denim against denim nearly electric. She could feel his eyes on her as he waited patiently for her to address the last two invitations.

And then he reached out and tucked the strands of hair behind her ear that had fallen against her cheek, exposing her neck to his gaze in the process. His fingers lingered for a few fretful heartbeats, then skimmed her jaw as his hand fell away.

A shiver coursed through her, and she calmly handed him the invitation and reached for the last one. "Am I boring you?"

"Not in the least." Without acknowledging that he'd touched her, he dampened a stamp and pressed it onto the corner of the envelope. "And why do I get the impression that you're disappointed about that fact?"

"More like amazed that you're actually enjoying this." Finished with the last invitation, she passed it to him to finalize the job. "Well, that's done." And now she could leave. "I'll drop them in the mail on my way home."

"All right." He gathered the other items for her to put into her tote bag, then stood, left the kitchen, and returned with her jacket, and a worn, masculine leather one.

Considering his sudden eagerness to help her clean up, and the fact that he was shrugging into his own jacket, she wondered if maybe she *had* waylaid his interest in party planning. Obviously, he had more exciting plans on his agenda, and was just politely going through the motions.

"Have you eaten anything?" he asked.

She grabbed her purse and tote bag and replied without thinking. "Not since breakfast."

"Me, either, and I'm starved. Come on, let's get out of here." He retrieved a set of keys off a hook on the nearby wall, and before she could gain her bearings, he had her hand enclosed in his and was guiding her out a back door to the garage.

He hit a button on the wall, a light went on, and the garage door started rolling upward, revealing a gray sky and snow flurries. A gleaming black Lexus with rich gold trim sat waiting, and Ryan opened the passenger door and ushered her into the butter-soft, tan leather interior.

Marveling at how easily he could manipulate her, how easily she let him, she buckled up while he circled around the car. Once he was behind the wheel, she asked, "Where are we going?"

The engine turned over on a soft purr of sound, and he glanced her way, grinning with wicked satisfaction. "On our first date."

3

"THIS IS NOT A DATE," Jessica reiterated once they'd arrived at the restaurant he'd selected and they'd placed their orders with the waitress.

Ryan glanced across the table at his *date*, and grinned. The sparkling laughter in her bright blue eyes belied her insistent tone and convinced him that she really didn't mind that he'd coerced her into having lunch with him. "You keep insisting that this isn't a date, but I think it all depends on how our afternoon ends."

Her features altered into mock suspicion. "What's the deciding factor?"

His gaze dropped to her soft lips, remembering the taste and lush feel of her. He could feast on her mouth for hours and still want more. "I think a kiss at the end of the day would determine whether this outing constitutes a date or not."

She dipped her head as she opened her napkin and spread it on her lap. "Sorry to disappoint you, Matthews, but this is strictly a *business* lunch."

He clasped his hands on the table and lowered his voice flirtatiously. "Ahh, but we haven't discussed any 'business' yet."

"But we *will*," she said, and dutifully pulled out her pad of paper and a pen, along with a very diligent attitude. "We need to nail down the specifics for the party so I can make the appropriate calls and get everything set up and scheduled."

"You win," he relented, feigning a defeated sigh. "Business it is. For today."

How was it that she looked both relieved *and* disappointed? The conflicting emotions he glimpsed intrigued him, and assured him that the potential for something more than their business dealings looked promising. It was just a matter of taking things slow and easy, and he had four weeks to persuade her to his way of thinking.

Admittedly, he'd never taken such time and care with a woman, but then the sophisticated, career-driven women he'd dated in the past had blatantly pursued *him*, and they'd both gone into the affair with the mutual understanding that there were no strings attached. Satiating physical needs had been the mainstay of those relationships, and ultimately their jobs had taken precedence over cultivating anything lasting. When they'd parted ways, they'd done so without regrets or emotional entanglements, and that type of arrangement had always suited him just fine.

Ever since meeting Jessica, he'd found himself growing more selective, to the point that he'd turned down a few offers from beautiful women he knew wouldn't make demands on his time. Attracting willing females had always come easily, but somewhere along the way indulging in a purely sexual relationship had lost its appeal.

Jessica stimulated not only his body, but his mind, and a woman hadn't accomplished such a feat in a long time, if ever. She made him think of things he'd put aside for his career, made him wonder if combining a real, lasting relationship with his job was do-able.

Made him wonder if there was some kind of way to strike a balance between achieving success and maintaining traditional values.

Not with her, his conscience mocked, reminding him of her ultimate aversion to his profession. She was tolerating him because of the party she wanted to throw for Brooke and Marc, and no doubt would say good riddance come New Year's Eve, unless he could convince her otherwise.

Yet there was no denying their attraction—or her reluctance to let their desire for one another take its natural course. And that meant he needed to help things along at a gradual, coaxing pace, in a way that would entice Jessica to give him a chance.

"...I thought appetizers would be more practical, instead of a full-course dinner," he heard Jessica say. "Quiches, chicken fingers, stuffed mushrooms, buffalo wings. Those kinds of things that everyone seems to like. I can call a few caterers, get their suggestions, too, and an estimate for the party." She took a drink of her soda, her gaze expectant. "What do you think?"

He pretended to mull over her suggestion. "That sounds fine to me."

"Great." Seemingly pleased with his easy acquiescence, she scribbled a note on a piece of paper with the heading "Caterer." Meanwhile the waitress arrived with their meal, setting a bowl of potato cheese soup in front of Jessica, and a cheeseburger in front of him.

They both started in on their respective lunches. After a few spoonfuls of soup, Jessica continued with her agenda. "I was going to contact Wilson's bakery to order a cake, and I was thinking we should go with white cake with a butter cream frosting."

He chewed on a bite of cheeseburger and thought

about her bland suggestion. Not wanting to outright discount her opinion, he chose his words carefully. "I'm not a cake connoisseur by any stretch of the imagination, but what's wrong with a flavored cake, like chocolate, or lemon, or even something more exotic like Black Forest?"

She wrinkled her nose at him, silently rejecting his idea. "Not everyone likes those flavors, and vanilla is pretty safe."

"But not very exciting or different," he pointed out, and saw her brows pucker ever so slightly at his argument. "I mean, why do we have to go with just one cake?"

"Because..." Her jaw snapped shut when no other words emerged, then she tried again. "Well, I just thought..." Seemingly unable to find a solid answer to dispute his creative concept, her shoulders slumped. "I guess we could get a variety," she said reluctantly. "What do *you* suggest?"

He'd put her on the defensive, and he hadn't meant to do that. And she obviously wasn't happy about his interference in *her* plans, but it just wouldn't be any fun if he gave in to her every whim without adding a little spice to the mixture. If it was really important, he'd let her have her way—but first, he'd prove to her that plain and practical white cake didn't compare to a more exciting, tasty and pleasurable array of desserts.

She was waiting for his ideas, very impatiently if the tapping of her pen was any indication. Keeping his expression unreadable, he dragged a French fry through a pool of ketchup and met her gaze from across the booth. "Can I have a few days to think about it?"

He'd definitely caught her off guard with his request to take the time to consider their cake dilemma. As much as he knew she would have preferred settling the issue here and now, she conceded to his request.

"Sure." She smiled as if to placate him. "Can you let me know your ideas and suggestions by the end of the week so we can make a decision and get the cake, or cakes, ordered?"

He nodded. "We'll definitely have it covered by the end of the week." And she'd have a new appreciation for the different tastes, flavors and textures of cake.

Closing her notepad, she stuffed it back into her tote bag in an attempt to terminate their discussion. He wasn't about to let her retreat so easily.

"You mentioned going in together on a gift for Brooke and Marc," he said, sucking off a smear of sauce from his thumb. "What did you have in mind?"

She dabbed at her mouth with her napkin as she swallowed a mouthful of soup. "I was thinking along the lines of something for their bathroom, which Brooke mentioned she wanted to redo in peach and greens. We could get them towels, a vanity set, a matching hamper—"

"Well, that's certainly very practical and sensible," he drawled, not at all impressed.

She bristled, a flicker of annoyance finally making an appearance in her gaze. "And what's wrong with that?"

"Nothing, I suppose, for old married couples." Done with his cheeseburger, he wiped his fingers on his napkin. "They're newlyweds, Jessie. Why not get them something fun and sexy for the bathroom?"

She stared at him as if he'd spouted Latin. "What in the world could be fun and sexy for the bathroom?"

Did she honestly have no clue? He shrugged, thinking of the things that would appeal to a woman, and a man, as well. "Lotions, candles and bath products. I've even seen some flavored finger paints that couples can use to rub all over each other's bodies, then lick off."

Her brows rose in skepticism, contradicting the flush stealing across her face. "You're kidding, right?"

He searched her flustered expression, and wondered about her sexual experience. She didn't strike him as completely innocent, but he was beginning to suspect that she'd never experimented beyond basic sex. Had she ever really been seduced by a man? *Really* seduced, in a way that encompassed every one of her five senses?

Bits and pieces of their conversation yesterday at his office filtered through his mind:

Chemistry is a great start.

Which rarely lasts once the relationship turns physical.

Is that your experience?

She hadn't given him an answer, but he was beginning to believe that her sexual encounters had been brief, and inadequate.

"It's a romantic and playful gift," he argued lightly. "Brooke and Marc would enjoy it. Any couple would."

"I doubt it."

Stubborn woman, he thought. She wouldn't doubt his choice if she knew just how sensual and erotic bathtime could be when you had someone to play with in the tub.

"Tell you what," he said, more than willing to compromise. "You purchase the practical items, and I'll buy the fun, sexy stuff. We'll put it all together and the gift will be a great combination of both."

She crossed her arms over her chest, her mouth pursed with frustration. No doubt she was wishing she'd never agreed to allow him to help with the party and planning.

"You're not convinced?"

"I just don't think your idea is a very *useful* gift, and it's not what I had in mind." Her tone was prim, but her words undercut him as a man who knew what women liked. "Maybe we ought to just buy our gifts separately."

Without further comment, he let the issue slide—for now. It appeared he had something else to teach her—about the many creative ways to enjoy being intimate. And when he was done with her, she'd gladly admit to his expertise.

THE MAN WAS INFURIATING!

Jessica walked into her apartment, yanked off her jacket, and released a loud, aggravated sound that did nothing to dispel the frustration coiling within her. Why couldn't Ryan just be a typical male and leave the plans for the New Year's Eve bash to her? Why did he have to put a crimp in her plans and suggestions?

And why did he have to be so gorgeous and sexy and make her want him so much when she knew how foolish any liaison with him would be?

She sank into the old, soft chair that had seen her through many years of pain, anger, tears and confusion. Though the sturdy frame had been reupholstered three times since her parents' divorce when she was nine years old, the chair was the one thing she couldn't part with from her childhood. The softness and warmth had become a comfort zone for her, a place that swallowed her up and offered silent solace for her troubles, whatever they were.

Like her disconcerting attraction to Ryan.

It was silly to hang on to the chair, she knew, considering all the bad memories that came with it—but it had been the one constant in her life, other than Brooke. When her father decided that he preferred the single life with a younger woman over the family he'd created, which entailed nearly destroying his wife in the process, Brooke had been the strong one during the turbulent divorce that had ensued. Brooke had taken care of her, and their mother. The separation had been a nasty one, with her father hiring a powerful attorney who had no compunction about taking advantage of her mother's emotional shock. And since her mother hadn't been able to afford to hire a decent lawyer for herself, she'd lost most everything to her husband and his new lover.

Bitter memories swamped Jessica as she remembered the years after the divorce, of her mother struggling to make ends meet because their father never paid child support and alimony on time, and Brooke sacrificing her teenage years to help raise her because their mother had to work two jobs to keep a roof over their heads, clothes on their backs, and food in their mouths.

An awful childhood, due to the abandonment of her father, and the insensitive, cruel nature of a divorce attorney more interested in his final take than a family's welfare.

She curled into the soft cushion and rubbed her hand over the powder-blue fabric. This chair had absorbed her tears and had taken all the angry pounding and abuse she would have unleashed on her father had he shown up to exercise his visitation rights. But ultimately, he hadn't cared for his daughters' emotional needs, just his own selfish desires. He'd never given a second thought to the family he'd left in shambles.

Neither had his cutthroat attorney.

When she thought of Ryan's profession, she thought of the lawyer who'd represented her father and coldly and cruelly demolished a little girl's dreams. A man who'd degraded a good wife and mother to benefit his client and pad his own pocketbook.

But Ryan wasn't cold and unfeeling and degrading. He was warm and caring and amusing, in a way that made her wonder how he was able to enjoy being a divorce attorney and accomplish all the necessary evils that went along with the profession when it was obvious that his own family ties were tightly woven. She wondered what had prompted his choice of occupation, then dismissed the thought because the answer really didn't matter—and *shouldn't* matter. Between his career and his drive and ambition, Ryan was completely wrong for her.

Closing her eyes, she burrowed her cheek against the plush headrest in an attempt to forget about her oppressive past, and the turbulent present. No matter the problems and afflictions that plagued her mind, the effect of the chair managed to calm her soul.

At the moment, Jessica was more concerned about the state of her heart...and Ryan Matthews easing his way into it. Despite everything he stood for, despite how frustrated and infuriated he'd made her today with the cake issue and his idea of a wedding present, she couldn't deny desiring Ryan Matthews, the man.

Her blossoming feelings for him were dangerous and could only lead to heartache. He himself had admitted that he wasn't looking for commitment, while she'd spent most of her adult life searching for just that, along with security and stability with a man. After living through her parents' nasty divorce, seeing her sister through a bad marriage, and making an error in judgment of her own in a previous relationship, Jessica was determined to make better choices. When she fell in love, she wanted it to last forever. When she married, she wanted to do it right the *first* time around.

And Ryan wasn't her vision of love and marriage material.

But he was a man who made her feel alive and desirable. He made her want to take risks and experience real passion. With him. The rest of the month stretched ahead of them, beckoning her to give in to that restless sensation swirling within her.

She drew a deep, shuddering sigh. She had no idea what she was going to do about her troubling attraction, and Ryan's unconcealed interest. She was struggling between holding on to her convictions, or letting go and tasting the bit of heaven his smiles, touches, and kisses promised.

She feared the latter was winning the battle.

But no matter what happened between her and Ryan, no matter if she surrendered to the attraction she was finding increasingly hard to resist, two things were certain. She was holding firm to her decision about ordering a single vanilla-flavored cake for the party, and no way was she going to be a part of his outrageous, unconventional bathroom gift!

THREE DAYS PASSED before Ryan called Jessica to discuss his thoughts on the cake issue. He meant to call sooner, but work and late-night preparations for court appearances had interfered with his good intentions.

While she wanted to settle the disagreement over the

phone, he'd insisted on coming by her place Thursday evening after dinner to resolve the matter—and made her suffer through another two days of wondering what he was up to and what he'd decided.

Finding a bakery who'd cater to his peculiar request hadn't been easy, thus part of the delay in seeing Jessica, but Ryan was confident that the end results of tonight's "taste test" would be worth the expense, and the wait. He planned to treat Jessica to her first seduction of her five senses.

After a long day filled with two depositions and a court appearance, Ryan headed home and changed from his suit into comfortable jeans and a long-sleeved cotton shirt. Heading down to the kitchen to heat up the leftover spaghetti he'd made the night before, he picked up Camelot along the way and gave her the attention she wanted, then treats when they reached the pantry. While his dinner heated and Camelot munched happily on her morsels, Ryan skimmed through the day's mail.

He set aside two utility bills, tossed out the junk mail, and opened a few Christmas cards from friends. At the bottom of the pile was a cream-colored envelope, his name and address printed with gold ink. At the sight of Haywood and Irwin's senior partner's name and *home* address affixed to the upper left-hand corner, a mixture of excitement, nerves, and anticipation swarmed in Ryan's belly.

Ripping open the envelope, he retrieved the engraved card inside. Elation bubbled within him as he read the contents. "I'll be damned," he murmured with a lopsided grin, feeling as though his six years of service and dedication to the firm, all his personal sacrifices, were finally paying off.

The gilded request invited him and a guest to the private, intimate Christmas gathering the senior partners held in appreciation of their most esteemed associates. Though the firm threw a casual office holiday party for all employees, only select members were invited to Haywood's home for the black-tie affair. It was an honor to be included in the elite group, a small but significant step up the corporate ladder, and it brought him one level closer to achieving his long-term goals. This was the first year they'd included him on their private guest list, and he wasn't about to refuse the opportunity to join the ranks of his other revered colleagues.

An RSVP card was included and requested notification of one or two guests. Anxious to respond favorably, he grabbed a pen from the holder on the counter near the phone, signed his name to the card, and moved to put an X on the line for one guest.

He hesitated. From what he'd heard and knew personally, the associates that attended Haywood's party brought their wives, or significant others. While he knew it wasn't a requirement that he bring someone to the event, he was also keenly aware that he was one of the few associates in the firm who was still a confirmed bachelor. No doubt, he'd be the only single and unattached employee in attendance.

The only person he'd consider taking was the only woman he had any interest in—Jessica. He imagined her in a room full of attorneys, and winced at the possibility of her cracking lawyer jokes and insulting the senior partners. But for all her joking and teasing with him, he'd like to believe she respected him enough not to undercut him in a professional atmosphere.

If she would even agree to accompany him to the party.

The idea of inviting Jessica definitely had merit. Not only would he have a beautiful, intelligent woman on his arm and wouldn't be the odd man out, it would also afford him the perfect opportunity to show her that attorneys were civilized people and not the ruthless savages she believed them to be.

Granted, there were lawyers who took advantage of people, as in any profession. He acknowledged that, but that wasn't why *he'd* chosen a career in law. Not only did he enjoy a solid debate, but his main goal had been to help people in need, in whatever capacity possible. And while he had some clients who were vicious and wanted revenge on their spouses, he always tried to look at a case objectively and fairly.

He wanted Jessica to treat him the same way.

Good luck in securing the date, Matthews, he thought cynically. That in itself would be an extraordinary achievement. Yet he wasn't ready to admit defeat without at least attempting to influence her into agreeing. He'd have his answer tonight.

The microwave beeped, signaling his dinner was warm. He ate a plate of spaghetti, headed back up to his bathroom to brush his teeth, then went to his closet. Flipping on the light, he perused his collection of silk ties and selected an odd patterned one he hadn't worn in years. He folded the strip of material and stuffed it into the front pocket of his jeans for later.

Then he left the house. He stopped at the bakery to pick up his order, and followed the directions Jessica had reluctantly given him to her complex. With a lightness to his step and the handle of a paper bag in each hand, he easily found Jessica's apartment and knocked.

She opened the door, dressed in white-washed jeans and a pale pink turtleneck, which was one of the most revealing things he'd ever seen on her. While the material covered her from wrists to throat, it was more snug than the loose sweaters and blouses she normally wore and revealed the full breasts that had pressed against his chest so deliciously that afternoon at his office.

Blocking his entrance, she crossed her arms over that lush chest, looking like a sentinel guarding priceless jewels. "I don't understand why we couldn't just handle this issue over the phone."

Knowing she'd discover his motives soon enough, he didn't bother to soothe her grumbles. Instead, he grinned, in too good a mood to let her complaint spoil what he had planned.

"Hello to you, too, Jessie." He stepped toward her, deliberately crowding her personal space. With his superior size, he forced her to back up and let him into her apartment, or end up pressed intimately against him.

With a startled gasp, she moved out of his way.

"Which way to the kitchen?" he asked, sending a quick glance around her place, which was decorated in pastels of blue, cream and bits of violet. Very soothing. Very feminine.

"Why?" She closed the door and eyed him suspiciously. "I already ate dinner."

"So did I." He lifted the bags, drawing her attention to the packages in his hands. "This is dessert."

Confusion colored her features, and obviously rendered her mute. Since she wasn't being a hospitable hostess, he headed toward the left, where he spied a small oak dining table, which led him right into the kitchen.

"I'm not in the mood for dessert, thank you," she said from behind him.

"Oh, you will be." Setting the bags on a wide chair, he stacked her quilted place mats to clear the surface of the table for their smorgasbord.

She came up beside him, and regarded his actions pensively. "I thought you were here to give me an answer on the kind of cake you think we should order."

"I am, not that what *I* think makes any difference to you and what you're determined to order." Done with his first task, he turned to look at her, letting a warm, lazy smile curve his lips. "You have it in that beautiful head of yours that being a *man* I haven't the slightest clue about cakes and desserts and what our guests might like."

A hint of a frown formed on her brows. "I never said that," she said quietly.

"Not in so many words, no, but you definitely thought it." He unloaded a number of small, square bakery boxes on the table, but left their lids secure. "I know you weren't thrilled with my suggestion of something other than plain ol' vanilla cake, so I'm here to convince you otherwise."

She stuffed her flattened hands into the back pockets of her jeans, drawing the material of her long-sleeved turtleneck tighter across her breasts. "What are you talking about?"

Masculine heat rushed through Ryan, followed by a sharp kick of desire. Judging by the faint outline of Jessica's nipples against soft cotton, Ryan guessed that she favored sheer, unpadded bras. There was nothing to conceal her body's natural response, and if he wasn't careful, his own unruly hormones were going to make his awareness of her just as obvious.

In an attempt to distract his thoughts he searched her kitchen drawers for a knife. "Out of necessity, I've become an authority on cakes, and when we're done sampling what I've brought, I'm confident that I'll have made an expert out of you, too."

She watched him set the knife on the table, then help himself to a chilled bottle of water from the refrigerator. "Ryan, you're not making any sense."

"It's simple, Jessie," he said, pushing up his shirt-sleeves to just below his elbow. "I've arranged a taste test of various cakes, and we'll see which one pleases your palate the most. And if vanilla still comes out as your top choice, we'll go with it." He rested his hands on her shoulders. "All I ask is that you give *my* flavors a fair chance."

She released a breath, and he reveled in the feel of the tension unfurling from her body. "All right," she agreed, and offered him a conciliatory smile.

Satisfied that he'd attained her cooperation, he patted the smooth, oak surface of the table. "I need you to sit right here."

"On the table?" she asked incredulously.

Unexpectedly, he touched her under the chin with his fingers, startling her. He gently lifted her gaze, so she had no choice but to look him directly in the eyes. Hers were so deep and blue he wanted to drown in their depths.

Very softly, imploringly, he said, "Just this once, make something easy on me, okay? And maybe you could trust me a little, too?"

He saw her internal struggle, and waited patiently,

knowing he couldn't do this unless he had her complete and total consent. After a few heartbeats, her expression softened in agreement, and she granted him the permission he sought by sliding her bottom onto the table where he'd indicated.

"Perfect," he murmured, then withdrew the tie from his front pocket. Gradually, he let it unravel. With mesmerizing slowness, he threaded the cool silk through his hands and fingers, and finally wrapped the tapered ends around his fists.

She dampened her bottom lip with her tongue as she watched him manipulate the strip of silk. He expected her to be nervous, and he supposed on some level *she* was uncertain, but there was no mistaking the glimmer of anticipation that darkened her eyes.

It was all the reassurance he needed.

Her gaze traveled from the taut fabric in his hands, to his face. "What do you intend to do with that tie?" she asked, her voice husky.

"I'm going to blindfold you."

4

JESSICA SHIVERED at the direct, male look in Ryan's deep brown eyes, the unmistakable seductive intent...but she wasn't afraid. She was suddenly very aware of the heat of his body, the reckless racing of her pulse, and the spiraling warmth settling low in her belly.

He loosened his hold on the tie, and the silk whispered through his long fingers again. The erotic sound strummed along her nerve endings just as effectively, awakening an undeniable excitement within her.

She struggled to draw a steady breath. For as titillating as she found his suggestion, she wasn't sure why shielding her vision was necessary. "Why do you need to blindfold me?"

"So you'll get the full effect of my experiment."

Stepping in front of her, he leaned forward to cover her eyes. When her locked knees brushed his groin, she automatically parted her legs to make room for him...and realized her mistake. He moved closer, nudging her thighs wider to accommodate his lean hips, making her far too aware of how intimate their position was.

Their close proximity didn't seem to bother him. "Being blindfolded will heighten your other senses, like the texture of the cake, the flavor, the smell. And I don't want you cheating and knowing ahead of time what you're tasting."

He wasn't proposing anything indecent, or sexual even, yet as darkness descended over her eyes and she felt his fingers tying a knot in the scrap of silk at the back of her head, a strange, forbidden thrill rippled through her. Once he had her blindfold secure, he gently tucked the sides of her hair behind her ears—to make sure the strands didn't get sticky with cake and frosting, she was guessing. But his touch lingered longer than necessary. His fingers traced the delicate, sensitive shell of her ears, and his knuckles lightly skimmed along her jaw.

Her breasts tightened in response to his caress, and she managed a breathless laugh. "Is touching me part of your experiment?"

"I'm just making sure your senses are alert."

Her senses were electrified, and more alive than they'd ever been before. And she had no idea where his eyes were, but she felt them *everywhere*. She resisted the urge to squirm.

"How many fingers am I holding up?" he asked.

A teasing smile touched the corner of her mouth. "Two and a half."

He chuckled, and the masculine timbre of that sound shimmied down her spine with impossible pleasure. "Good. Your vision is definitely impaired."

He moved away for a moment, she heard a box opening and other sounds she couldn't identify, and then he returned to the cove between her thighs.

"Here's the first one," he said, and brushed her bottom lip with the confection.

She parted her lips at his urging and took a dainty bite of what he offered. Immediately, she identified it as the white cake. It was moist with a buttercream frosting...and very ordinary tasting. She kept her revelation to herself, still believing vanilla was their safest bet to please thirty people.

"This is the vanilla for sure," she said as she chewed and swallowed. "Are you eating it, too?"

"I'll skip this one." Another box opened. "I already know how bland and boring vanilla is."

She wrinkled her nose at him. "I can hardly wait to taste what *you* selected. Fruitcake, maybe?"

That deep, rich laugh again. And then two things assailed her senses at the same time as he took his place in front of her. The delectable fragrance of chocolate, and a burning sensation where he rested his palm on her thigh. The combination nearly short-circuited her central nervous system.

With effort, she concentrated on the scent wafting beneath her nose. "Chocolate?" she guessed.

"Ahh, but this isn't your ordinary chocolate cake."

She inhaled deeply, catching a whiff of something richer and more decadent. Since he wasn't forthcoming with the flavor, she sampled it for herself. Cocoa, a hint of coffee in the frosting and filling, and chocolate mocha candy shavings that all but melted in her mouth.

"Oh, wow," she murmured appreciatively. She licked a crumb from the corner of her mouth, feeling ravenous and greedy. "Can I have another bite?"

"I thought you might like that one." He fed her another morsel, and slowly dragged his fingers along her lower lip. "It's called Chocolate Mocha Rapture."

Rapture. Her eyes rolled heavenward. Oh, yeah, she'd definitely been transported to another plane. Her body felt flushed, drugged, heavy. *Aroused.*

He pressed a chilled plastic bottle in her hand and urged it up to her mouth. "Take a drink to cleanse your palate. I don't want anything to taint the next flavor."

Though the water was cold and refreshing sliding down her throat, it did nothing to extinguish the flames Ryan's "experiment" had ignited. Setting the bottle next to her on the table, she waited anxiously for the next dessert.

"Now here we have something sweet and *very* sinful."

Her nostrils flared as a luscious aroma consumed her senses. Her stomach rumbled, and she licked her lips in anticipation.

"Open up," he murmured.

She did, and groaned as an exquisite flavor filled her mouth. Ripe strawberries. Whipped cream filling. A light, fluffy frosting. Shavings of white chocolate. She was certain she'd died and gone to heaven.

"More?" he asked, seemingly knowing exactly what she liked.

She nodded, beyond caring that she wanted to overload her senses with the lush sensuality of Ryan's taste test, or that he'd probably gloat later over proving his point that vanilla was a bland choice. She'd never savored such divine recipes, never felt so seduced by tastes and textures.

"Please," she said, parting her lips for him. She took such a huge, devouring bite that the cream filling oozed out of the middle. Instinctively, she lifted her hand to stop the flow, and by luck caught the dollop in her palm, but not before she'd smeared it along her chin, too.

"Argh." The sound of distress caught in her throat. Then, unable to help herself, she laughed with frivolous lightness. "I'm making a mess. I hope you brought napkins."

"Don't need 'em," he replied, his voice infused with

amusement, and something far more mischievous. "I'll take care of the spills and leftovers."

She assumed he meant to clean up later when they were done, so she wasn't prepared for his more resourceful method. He caught her wrist and she nearly jumped out of her skin when she felt his warm mouth nibble off the portion of cake stuck to her palm. A hot ache spread through her as his teeth grazed her flesh, and she all but melted when he thoroughly laved her fingers, then flicked his tongue wickedly along the crevices between. And when he was done with her hand, he went to work on her chin, eating the crumbs and licking away the frosting and filling with agonizingly slow laps of his tongue.

He indulged in her as if *she* were dessert.

"Delicious, and so sweet," he murmured, his low voice vibrating against her cheek.

A sultry pressure coiled low as she waited anxiously for him to complete his task and make his way to her mouth and kiss her deeply...

It never happened. As if he hadn't completely turned her inside out with wanting, he moved away and returned to the business at hand, selecting another cake for her to try. This one was Butter Brickle Ecstasy, and it was everything the name implied...pure, unadulterated bliss for the taste buds.

With each sampling, he tempted and teased her, and she luxuriated in the provocative pleasures he evoked. He used his lips and tongue to clean up the sticky messes she deliberately made, yet always stopped short of kissing her mouth.

Frustration nipped at her. She wanted to take off the blindfold and participate without hindrance—and entice him in return. He insisted it remain, or the experiment ended.

He won, because she wasn't ready or willing to forfeit the delightful confections still to come.

He went on to feed her Fuzzy Navel Cake drenched with peach schnapps that she couldn't seem to get enough of, and a melt-in-your-mouth champagne cake with French buttercream frosting that made her feel giddy and drunk—not on alcohol, but the insatiable desire he was gradually building within her.

But it was the last selection that completely undid her: moist chocolate cake layered with chocolate mousse, drizzled with creamy caramel, and topped with a cloud of whipped cream and chunks of butter toffee. This cake was gooey, messy, but a sumptuous feast that tantalized her mouth and pleased her belly.

She moaned deep in her throat as the contents dissolved on her tongue and slid down her throat like honeyed silk. "This cake is *incredible*. What is it called?"

He offered her another bite, knowing from previous requests that she wouldn't settle for just one taste. "Would you believe the bakery called it Better Than Sex Cake?"

She licked the corner of her mouth, not wanting to spare even a smudge of whipped cream, caramel, or chocolate mousse. "Oh, God, they're right." She sighed in undisguised gratification. "This is almost... *euphoric*."

"Do you really think it's that much better?" he asked, his tone dubious.

"In my experience, yeah," she said, realizing too late just how much she'd revealed.

There was a pause, then, "This cake, no matter how

incredible, doesn't compare to the real thing...not when you're with the right person."

And her one and only lover obviously hadn't been that right person. Suddenly feeling self-conscious under Ryan's scrutiny, she decided it was time to end their playful game, and reached for the blindfold to remove it from her eyes.

His fingers gently encircled her wrist, stopping her before she could tug the tie loose. His touch was firm, hot, branding her.

"Not yet," he said in a low, sexy voice. "Maybe you'd like more?" His comment was double edged, giving her the distinct impression that he was referring to more than just feasting on the exotically named cake she'd just eaten. "It's right here, Jessie, in the palm of my hand. Just reach out and take it, and the euphoria can be all yours. As much as you like, for as long as you want."

Cocooned in darkness, stimulated by his words and the sexual slant of their conversation, Jessica's heart beat erratically in her chest. He'd issued her a subtle dare, a flagrant invitation...beckoning her to give in to her secret desires and experience just how good sex, with the right person, could be.

She swallowed to ease the tightness in her throat. "I don't want to eat the cake alone," she whispered.

"I don't like to eat my cake alone, either," he said, humor and understanding mingling. "How about we share it, then?"

"All right," she agreed.

Standing between her legs again so she was surrounded by his scent and heat, he took her hand and slowly guided it to the side where the cakes were displayed. She had no idea what he intended, but entrusted herself to him and followed his lead.

She sucked in a quick, startled breath as he eased her fingers into the soft, silky layers of cake—all the way up to her knuckles. His own hand slid along hers as he encouraged her to play in the ingredients and feel the various textures, all of which had suddenly become very intoxicating to her senses.

Her entire body tingled with a strange excitement. "This feels..."

"Arousing?" he suggested.

Oh, yeah, definitely that. She grinned, not sure she was ready to admit just how much his provocative demonstration was affecting her. "I was thinking more along the lines of squishy."

He chuckled. "Then maybe we need to alter your way of thinking." He entwined their fingers, tangled them sensuously, using the mousse, caramel, and whipped cream to lubricate the rhythmic slide of his fingers between hers. He leaned into her, so his lips grazed her ear. "*This* is how good sex feels with the right person...slippery, sensual, *erotic.*"

She bit her lower lip as an illicit, liquid warmth cascaded over her and pooled between her thighs. She had no choice but to believe him. She *wanted* to believe that making love could be so thrilling, so impetuous, so rapturous.

Too soon, he lifted his hand from hers, slowly dragging it out of the cake and away. She flinched in startled surprise when his sticky, gooey fingers touched her mouth.

"And this is how good sex *tastes*," he murmured huskily as he smeared the luscious concoction along her bottom lip. "Sweet, heady, *euphoric.* Taste it, Jessie, and see for yourself."

His sexy words tempted her. Unable to stop herself, her tongue darted out, slowly licking away the confection.

This is how good sex tastes.

His promise rumbled through her mind, and suddenly, one taste wasn't enough. "I want more," she said in a low, breathy voice.

His finger returned, gently pressing down on her bottom lip until they parted and she took him inside the damp heat of her mouth. Removing her own hand from the cake, she grabbed his wrist so he couldn't pull back while she tormented him the same way he'd done to her. Heedless of the mess they were smearing everywhere, she nibbled the chocolate and caramel from his fingers, then leisurely stroked and swirled her tongue along each individual digit in an instinctive, up-and-down rhythm. She felt him shudder and heard him let out a hiss of breath in response.

She heard him swear, felt him try and tug his hand back, but she held firm. Her hunger had become a rapacious thing, and it wasn't for cake and sweets, but for the need to experience *slippery, sensual, erotic sex.* With Ryan.

She felt his body shift in front of her, wedging himself more intimately between her thighs, and then his mouth was on hers, urgent and insistent, and she relinquished his fingers for the pleasure of his kiss.

And from there, everything went wild and out of control. He swept an arm around her back and hauled her up against his body, forcing her legs wider to accommodate his hips and the unyielding press of his fierce erection against her aching cleft. They were fused from lips to thighs, and she still wasn't close enough.

Spearing her cake-encrusted fingers into the warm, thick hair at the nape of his neck, she arched into him, opening her mouth wider beneath his to accept the hot, sexual thrusts of his tongue. One of his hands mimicked her move, cupping the back of her head, threading through the hair that wasn't restrained by the blindfold. The fingers of his other hand caressed her jaw, her throat, and skimmed lower until he held the full weight of her breast in his palm. He kneaded the mound of flesh, searing her with breath-taking heat. His thumb flicked across the diamond-hard nipple straining against her cotton shirt, plucked the tip delicately, and a needy moan escaped her.

Feverish desire clawed at her, submersing her deeper under Ryan's spell. Being blindfolded and ravished was like being swept up into a dark, forbidden fantasy. The thrill of it was liberating.

Unexpectedly, he lifted his lips from hers, putting her system in immediate withdrawal. Their breath mingled in rapid bursts, and he threw her off-kilter again when he pressed an achingly light and tender kiss to the corner of her mouth. "Go out with me," he rasped.

"No," she groaned automatically, so used to rejecting him that it had become second nature.

He swooped in for another kiss, this one slower than the last, more persuasive, more possessive. "One date," he uttered once he let her up for air.

Her resolve crumbled a fraction. "Maybe."

He took her under again, thoroughly consuming her mouth until her lips felt swollen and devoured. He brushed his knuckles over her erect nipples, teasing and tormenting her. He moved on, trailing kisses along her jaw. His fingers pulled down the collar of her turtleneck so he had access to nuzzle her throat.

She shuddered uncontrollably at the hot, wet glide of his tongue across her skin, and whimpered as he drew her flesh between his teeth for a love bite.

"Dinner and drinks." His hoarse, urgent whisper scalded her ear. "Say yes, Jessie."

Dizzy from the blindfold, faint and flushed from his sensual assault, she obeyed his command. *"Yes."*

She stiffened, just as the phone on the kitchen counter rang.

Oh, God, had she really surrendered and said yes to Ryan Matthews?

The phone pealed again. She didn't move, and neither did Ryan, though she could hear his heavy, labored breathing, could feel the virile heat radiating off him, and smell what she now knew was the scent of good sex...*sweet, heady, euphoric.*

Silently, she cursed the blindfold that had completely stripped away her restraints and inhibitions. Unable to see Ryan, her feminine wants and needs had taken precedence over the fact that this man before her was all wrong for her.

Her answering machine clicked on, and her voice echoed in the quiet kitchen with a brief outgoing message, followed by a shrill beep.

"Hi, Jess, it's Brooke," her sister said, sounding upbeat and cheerful. "I received an invitation in the mail today for a New Year's Eve party at Ryan Matthews', and I'm assuming you got one, too. I also wanted to talk to you about Christmas. Give me a call tonight at home or tomorrow at the office. Love ya."

The line disconnected, and the answering machine clicked off.

Unexpected guilt swamped Jessica, as if her sister had personally caught her in a naughty act. And she was very naughty for consorting with the enemy, for allowing him to breach her well-constructed barriers. With pleasure infusing her veins, she'd forgotten one important issue while he'd coaxed her into agreeing to go out on a date with him—she didn't like divorce attorneys.

But she liked Ryan. Wanted him. Desired him.

His long fingers slipped beneath the band of silk concealing her vision and lifted it over her head. She squinted as the bright kitchen light pierced her eyes and her pupils contracted. Gradually, her gaze focused. On the man standing in front of her, who was watching her guardedly. On the disarray of baked goods around the table. Crumbs littered the table, the floor, and her jeans. There was cake and filling everywhere—on his shirt, his face, arm, and hands. She hadn't survived the attack, either. Her cheek was sticky, as were her fingers. And she had a white handprint on her shirt, outlining her breast.

She dragged a shaky hand through her hair, and winced as her fingers tangled in a clump of frosting stuck to the strands. "What a mess..." *she'd made of things,* her conscience finished for her.

Oh, Lord, staring into his intense, deep-brown eyes, she was so utterly confused. Undoubtedly, her emotions were tangled up in the passion he inspired, making her forget all the reasons why it would be so foolish to let herself get any more involved with him.

She fabricated a smile. "You win," she conceded, scooting off the table.

He stepped to the side out of her way, but continued to eye her cautiously, as if he knew just how skittish she'd become now that she'd had time to assess what they'd done. "What's the prize?"

"Proving me wrong." Desperately, she tried to affect a business demeanor, which was difficult to do when her body still throbbed and ached for something that would never happen with Ryan.

Slippery, sensual, erotic sex.

She pressed a hand to still the fluttering in her belly at that thought, and smudged more frosting on her clothing. She grimaced. She needed a shower, and she needed distance from this man who threatened everything from her sanity to her beliefs.

"Vanilla is by far the most bland and boring cake I've ever tasted," she admitted, knowing it would be ridiculous for her to say otherwise, not after being such a glutton with the flavors he'd brought. "How about we order three of those cakes. Is that variety enough for you?"

"Sure." He didn't smirk or exult over the fact that he'd gained her acquiescence. Instead, he tipped his head, regarding her with warm concern. "You pick which ones."

Ignoring the silent question in his eyes that asked if she was okay, she glanced at the assortment of half-eaten desserts on the table. She was far from okay, but she'd be much better once he left and she scrambled to put her priorities back in line.

Which didn't include *slippery, sensual, erotic sex* with Ryan Matthews.

Selecting only three flavors was a difficult task, especially when they'd all been so delicious. "How about we go with strawberries and cream, the champagne cake, and butter brickle?" She deliberately kept the names short and precise, without the sexy labels he'd used to describe them.

"Good choices," he said as a too-intimate smile curved his mouth. "Though I think the Better Than Sex Cake would be a great conversation piece for the guests."

Unwilling to let him think she couldn't handle ordering that particular cake because of the sensual memories it evoked, she gave an uncaring shrug. "I'll add it to the order."

An awkward silence fell between them, rife with sexual and emotional undercurrents—neither of which Jessica wanted to bring out in the open and discuss.

She grappled for an excuse to end the evening with Ryan. "I, uh, need to take a shower. I have frosting and cake everywhere." She waved a hand toward the mess on the table. "Just leave everything and I'll clean it up later. When you're done washing up, lock the door behind you."

Without giving him an opportunity to reply or a chance to postpone his departure, she made a beeline down the hall and sought the private sanctuary of her bedroom.

RYAN RELEASED a long stream of breath that did little to ease the self-reproach twisting inside him. He wasn't going anywhere, not until he'd cleaned up the mess *he'd* made of things. With Jessica.

He'd rushed her. Overwhelmed her. And that had never been his intent. He'd merely meant to show her how fantastic the chemistry was between them, and open her up to the possibility of giving him a fair chance at being something more than a party-planning buddy.

She'd definitely been a willing partner in what had transpired on this very table—lush, wanton and uninhibited. Her compliance had been genuine, her enthusiastic response to his kisses and caresses unfeigned. But her body and mind weren't in harmony, and that was the crux of their problem.

While his seductive demonstration had succeeded in stripping Jessica of her physical reserve, it hadn't completely diminished her reluctance to trust him. She harbored doubts and fears that stretched beyond wallowing in sexual gratification. And for a reason that he hadn't completely sorted out yet in his own head, he *wanted* her trust—just as much as he wanted to make love to her and introduce her to all the pleasures she'd been denied.

He knew if he left now as she'd insisted, he'd give her the perfect opportunity to retreat and shore up those defenses of hers. And that wouldn't do. He'd merely scratched the surface of Jessica's complexities, and he wasn't through discovering the depth of those fascinating layers.

With his next strategy filtering through his mind, he set about tidying up the kitchen. Most of the small cakes were destroyed from their taste test, and weren't worth saving. He tossed the remnants and boxes in the trash, wiped down the table, and picked up the crumbs that had fallen on the floor. Then he went into the bathroom he found off the living room and scrubbed his hands and arms free of dried frosting and cake. He rinsed the confection from his face, and decided there wasn't anything he could do about his hair until he took his own shower at home.

If things had ended more positively, he might be sharing Jessica's shower with her, he thought with a rueful smile at himself in the mirror. The image of her naked and wet, with water sluicing down the sleek curves she hid, invaded his musings. The vivid fantasy caused a liquid heat to rush to his groin. He swore and splashed cold water over his face.

A half an hour later, Jessica finally exited her bedroom and found him reclining against the tiled counter with a bottle of cold water in his hand, and the kitchen spotless.

She came to an abrupt stop when she saw him. Wariness instantly colored her eyes, made more strikingly blue by her freshly scrubbed face and the damp strands of honey-blond hair falling haphazardly to her shoulders. She wore an old terry robe that swallowed her up in the folds of worn material, from neck to ankles. On her feet were a pair of pink house slippers.

And in that moment, she appeared incredibly vulnerable to him.

Then her chin lifted a stubborn notch, reminding him of the spitfire he was used to dealing with. "You're still here," she said, her voice indicating her surprise. "I told you it wasn't necessary for you to clean up."

He shrugged a shoulder. "I contributed to the mess. It was the least I could do." Finished with his water, he tossed the plastic bottle into the recycle bin under the sink, then resumed his position against the counter.

"Well, thank you for your help." *And now you're free to leave*, her tone silently added.

"You're welcome." He didn't budge.

She released an exasperated sound beneath her breath, and tugged on the sash to her robe, tightening it around her slender waist. The lapels billowed open slightly, affording him a tantalizing glimpse of smooth skin and the beginning slope of one breast. He wondered if she was completely naked beneath the terry material, and resisted the urge to reach out, untie her belt, and find out for himself...

She crossed her arms over her chest and cleared her throat, effectively drawing his attention upward. Her eyes flared with impatience...and awareness. "Ryan...it's getting late, and you really should go."

"In a minute," he said in a slow, deliberate drawl. "You owe me something, and I didn't want to leave without it."

"Money for the cakes?" She asked the question in such a hopeful way that he knew she'd purposely misconstrued his meaning. She moved past him to open a drawer beneath the counter, leaving a scented trail of jasmine in her wake. "I don't have any extra cash on me, but I'd be happy to write you a check—"

He grabbed her hand before she could retrieve her checkbook, and closed the drawer with a bump of his hip. He waited until she looked up at him. "I don't want your money, Jessie. I want *you*," he said softly, sincerely. "And you owe me a date."

She extricated her arm from his grasp. "You obtained that date under duress, *counselor*."

He couldn't contain the laugh that escaped him. "You call the way you kissed me *duress?*"

Her mouth pursed, and he was half-tempted to haul her up against him and kiss her senseless again, until she melted and admitted the truth—that she'd been a willing participant in what had taken place on the table behind her.

"I certainly wasn't in the right frame of mind to

make any kind of decision, and being the lawyer you are, you took advantage of that fact."

He shook his head at her reasoning, seeing it for the excuse it was, and a poor one at that. "So, does this mean you're reneging on your promise?"

She picked at a piece of lint on her sleeve, her gaze downcast, her voice resigned. "I think you and I ought to just stick to party planning."

In his estimation, they'd gone too far to backpedal to platonic friends. Yet it was obvious that he still needed to tread slowly and cautiously with her. "Would you go out with me in the guise of doing me a favor?"

That captured her attention. She lifted her head and met his gaze, waiting to hear his proposition.

"I *do* need a date," he inhaled, taking a huge leap of faith, "for my firm's Christmas party."

Her incredulous expression told him his risk hadn't paid off. "Me? In a room full of lawyers?" She flattened a hand to her chest, her eyes wide, and visibly shuddered. "No, thank you."

"One date," he said, not ready to give up just yet. "No strings attached. I swear it."

A slow, devious smile played around the corner of her mouth. "How do you know when a lawyer is lying?"

Having been the recipient of that particular joke before, he knew the punch line. "His lips are moving," he replied with a grin.

"*Exactly*," she said, obviously believing he was weaving a fib of his own.

He grabbed the tail end of her sash and gave it a playful tug. "Aw, come on, Jessie," he said in a low, deep voice. "You know you want to accept...maybe just a little?"

She shook her head adamantly and pushed her hands into the side pockets of her robe. "Not only am I refusing for personal reasons, I don't do fancy, schmancy parties. I'm sure it won't be difficult for you to find some other willing female to adorn your arm."

He still held on to the belt of her robe, suspecting if he let go she'd bolt. And he wanted to keep her near. "I asked *you* because I don't want to go with anyone else." And that was the truth, whether she believed him or not.

"Then it looks like you'll be attending solo." The barest hint of regret tinged her voice. "I'm sorry, Ryan...I *can't* do it. It's those personal ethics of mine and all. You understand."

Her excuse was a familiar one, but this time he wasn't going to accept her obscure argument, not when he suddenly had more at stake than just securing a date to his firm's holiday party—like securing her trust. "The thing is, Jessie, I don't understand those personal ethics of yours. Not completely. It has to do with me being a divorce attorney, that I know, but *why?*"

She didn't reply. Instead, he watched those defenses of hers slowly rise, saw it in the stiffening of her spine and the guarded look in her eyes, and knew if he didn't act fast he'd lose the opportunity to reach beyond those barriers she was about to erect.

He wove his fingers casually through the end of her sash, keeping her close. "How is it that you can respond to me the way you did earlier, so openly and honestly, yet shut me out emotionally? I can't help but take that personally, Jessie."

She swallowed, hard, but her gaze remained steady on his. "I apologize if you feel that I led you on."

"No, I don't feel that way at all." He smiled gently. "I think you're scared, and maybe confused, and that's okay. But I think I've earned the right to know *what* you're afraid of."

Her chin lifted a notch, but she appeared more vulnerable than mutinous. "All right. I'm very attracted to you, but beyond the physical attraction, I'm having a difficult time getting past what you do for a living, and everything it implies."

He'd known his occupation posed a problem for her from the very beginning, but he wanted deeper knowledge. "You mean me being a divorce attorney?" he asked, coaxing her to open up even more.

"That's part of it," she said, nodding guardedly. "I'm not fond of divorce attorneys. I saw firsthand with my mother and father just how cold and calculating people in that profession can be. I watched my father's cutthroat lawyer nearly destroy my mother, and rip apart our family, all for his client's benefit. My mother struggled for years after the divorce just to make ends meet, while my father walked away with a nicely padded bank account and a charming new life without any familial responsibilities."

Her words didn't paint a flattering picture at all, and made his heart go out to the little girl who'd witnessed that devastating separation, and to the woman who was still affected by her father's abandonment. "And that's what you think I do for a living?"

"Don't you?" The challenge in her voice was unmistakable.

He paused. How to explain without incriminating himself? "What happened to your mother, your family, was very unfortunate, but there're always two sides to every case. And while some divorces aren't pleasant and amicable, I try to look at all my cases objectively and represent my clients to the best of my ability, with *facts*."

"Even if that means ruining the other person's life in the process?"

"Sometimes I represent that defendant, and women like your mother who struggle not to get shafted by their conniving husbands. It all depends on the couple and circumstances involved. Some cases are simple and friendly. Others are ugly and vicious. I have no control over the personality types I represent, and trust me when I say that there are *all* kinds."

She stepped away, and he released his hold on her sash, suspecting that she needed the emotional distance. He was stunned by the depth to which Jessica was affected by her parents' divorce. It was evident that she carried the bitterness of a childhood gone bad, and that her experiences had caused her to be wary and cautious, not just of divorce attorneys, but of men in general.

From across the kitchen, she slanted him a curious look. "So, you actually enjoy what you do?"

He slid his fingers into the front pockets of his jeans as he mulled that over, thinking about the past six years of his career, the highlights and the frustrating cases he'd had to represent. "Most of the time, I do. I'll admit that sometimes I'll take on a case that's mentally draining, but I love the challenge of my job, and the complexities involved." He thought of his long-term intentions, and shared those, too. "I'm working towards being a junior partner, and possibly heading up the family law department at Haywood and Irwin. But the main reason I chose a career in law was to help people."

The corner of her mouth quirked with a smile. "Why not be a doctor then?"

"I thought about it," he replied honestly. "But when I almost threw up while dissecting a frog in high school biology I knew I'd never make it through med school. I'm too squeamish when it comes to blood and guts." He grinned in amusement and saw her bite the inside of her cheek to keep from laughing. "So, instead, I concentrated my efforts on the debate team, and discovered that I really enjoyed disputing issues and trying to sway people to agree with my ideals and opinions."

"Which you're very good at," she admittedly wryly.

He tipped his head, acknowledging the backhanded compliment. "Yet I can't seem to convince you to go out on a date with me, or accompany me to my firm's Christmas party."

She exhaled a slow breath, and combed her fingers through her still damp hair. "Ryan...what you do for a living goes against what I believe in. Despite what my mother went through with my father, and Brooke's own divorce, I still believe in love, marriage, and happily-ever-afters. It's what I want for myself one day, with the right person."

And she obviously didn't consider him a candidate for the position. Her argument was solid and indisputable. And as much as he was attracted to her, as much as he was coming to care about her, he couldn't offer her the kind of promises she demanded, and deserved. She'd given him every reason to take a huge step back, to leave her alone, but he discovered he couldn't do it, because for the first time in his adult life, he wanted to take that huge step *forward* with a woman...and see where it all might lead.

A scary prospect, even for him. But after a year of

wanting Jessica, his gut twisted into a giant knot at the thought of completely severing all ties with her.

Armed with a new determination, he took that step forward, moving toward her, and she watched him close the distance between them. He smiled, and attempted to dispel the gloom their conversation had cast over the room. "Are you *sure* you won't consider coming to that Christmas party? It might give you a whole different perspective on lawyers."

"I doubt it. I think it would be smarter, and safer, if I didn't attend something as important as your firm's Christmas party with you."

Unwilling to admit defeat just yet, he tried a different approach. "I know I hit you with this unexpectedly, and I really didn't give you the chance to consider your answer—"

"I won't change my mind, Ryan," she said, firmly cutting off his entreaty.

"I'd like to think you will." He dared to reach out and touch her, gently stroking his thumb along her cheek. A sense of satisfaction filled him when she didn't retreat. "Just think about it, okay?"

And in the meantime, if the only way to dissolve her defenses was to use seduction, then they'd at least enjoy themselves in the process.

5

JESSICA SAT IN FRONT of her computer, unable to concentrate on the medical reports she needed to transcribe for the doctors that employed her services. Thanks to Ryan's parting remark the night before, she couldn't think about anything else except his invitation to his firm's Christmas party.

She'd told him no, and meant it. She'd told him she wouldn't change her mind, and she meant that, too. She couldn't envision herself in a room crowded with attorneys, smiling and trying to make polite small talk and acting as though she approved of what they did for a living. She harbored too many resentments and bitter memories to advocate the legal profession, especially those who represented divorce cases and went against their opponent with greedy intent.

What Ryan was suggesting was ludicrous, and impossible. The complications of involving herself with him on such a personal level had the potential to break her heart. Not only was his career choice a problem for her, but his aspirations didn't leave much room in his life to devote to building a lasting relationship. Nothing permanent could come of them being together.

She *knew* that, so why couldn't she just consider Ryan a friendly acquaintance and keep their association at that?

Slippery, sensual, erotic sex.

She groaned as those words echoed in her mind, as they had all night long and into the early morning hours. Yeah, she admitted that particular promise had something to do with her preoccupation with Ryan. He'd shown her a glimpse of that temptation, and she'd be lying if she said she didn't want to experience the full spectrum of pleasure he'd introduced her to, and take those voluptuous sensations to their inevitable conclusion.

There was no denying she was itching to try something new, to be a little rebellious and break past the caution that had ruled most of her life. She'd been a good girl for so long, and now she wanted to live a little, embrace the passion Ryan evoked, and see where it all led.

She sighed, her belly clenching with desire as she recalled the skillful range with which Ryan had used his mouth on hers. Whether long, slow and lazy, or deep, hungry and rapacious, his kisses had the ability to bring her to a fever pitch of excitement in no time flat. Her lashes fluttered closed as she imagined his mouth elsewhere, and her breasts swelled in response to the visual fantasy. She bit her bottom lip, aching to feel the heat of his breath on her skin, the silky stroke of his tongue across her tight, sensitive nipples, the wet suction of his mouth closing over her...

The phone on her desk rang, startling her out of her reverie and setting her heart to a frantic pace. Last night before he'd left her place, Ryan had told her he had a long, busy day at the office today, and had catch-up work to handle on Saturday, so he wouldn't be able to see her until Sunday. He'd requested she come by his house on Sunday so they could finalize the menu and other party matters, so she wasn't expecting him to call. She *knew* he was busy with work, and was irritated with herself for wanting it to be him on the phone.

Forcing the gorgeous, sexy rogue from her mind, she picked up the line and answered with a breathless, "Hello?"

"Hey, Jess, did you forget about me?"

Jessica winced. Her sister. She'd been too distracted by the results of Ryan's cake seduction, then their discussion, to return her call last night. And today, well, she was still distracted. "Actually, I was just going to call you back."

"I guess I saved you the dime. Where were you last night when I called?" Brooke asked, displaying those protective sister instincts that she'd honed since the age of thirteen.

Tasting a slice of euphoria. "I, uh, was having dessert with a friend."

The excuse slipped from her tongue, as truthful as she'd allow. Including the fact that Ryan had been her companion for the evening would only serve to rouse Brooke's curiosity, and promote questions she didn't want to answer. Once the New Year's Eve surprise reception was over, her contact with Ryan would return to a minimum, as it had always been. As it should be. And her sister would never have to know that her association with Ryan while planning the party had included his thrilling attempts at seduction.

"Well, I hope you had a fun time."

Sexy, sinful fun.

Knowing she'd never get any work done this morning, she saved and shut down the document she'd been typing, and turned the conversation to the reason why Brooke had called. "You mentioned that you received an invitation for a New Year's Eve party at Ryan's,'' she said lightly, careful not to give any part of the surprise away. "Are you planning on going?"

"Yeah, it sounds like a fun way to bring in the New Year. How about you? Are you going to go?"

She grinned at her sister's assumption, and affected a convincing reluctance on her end. "What makes you think I'd get an invitation, too? I mean, Ryan is *Marc's* friend, and it's not as though he and I are exactly buddies."

Last night, they'd come damn close to being lovers.

"Oh, come on, Jess," Brooke replied in a teasing tone. "Both Marc and I agreed that Ryan wouldn't pass up the opportunity to see you. If he's having a party, you'd be invited."

Except the whole entire party had been her idea, and if anything, *she'd* invited *Ryan*. "I was invited," she admitted, playing along for her sister's benefit.

"And?"

"I haven't RSVP'd yet," she said, forcing an indecisive tone to her voice. It wouldn't do to let her sister think she was anxious.

"Say yes," Brooke encouraged. "It'll be fun and you'll have a good time."

Say yes. Ryan's invocation last night whispered through her conscience, as did her pitifully easy surrender. And she *had* reneged on her promise, but with good reason.

She shook the incident from her mind, determined to put it behind her. "All right, I'll go," she said, coiling the stretchy phone cord around her finger. "Besides, it might be a great way to meet someone new and interesting."

Brooke laughed. "I doubt that's why Ryan invited

you, but I'll let the two of you work that out at the party."

Jessica let the implication in her sister's comment slide. Over the past year, her sister had witnessed many encounters between her and Ryan, the sparks and teasing and flirting, as well as the attraction she'd fought to keep at bay. And in a matter of a week, Ryan had chiseled through those carefully constructed defenses. Shoring them back up after last night was more difficult than she'd imagined.

She rocked back in her chair. "So, how's married life?"

"Blissful." A content sigh echoed over the phone lines. "Absolutely wonderful."

Jessica smiled. Her sister's relationship with Marc Jamison hadn't been easy at first, and certainly had been complicated, but with the respect and love the two shared they'd managed to work through the issues and problems that had stood in their way.

"I'm glad everything worked out with Marc," she said sincerely. Her sister's first marriage had been less than ideal, and it warmed Jessica that Brooke had found a man who was her equal. It gave her hope for herself. "He's a great guy, and you deserve to be happy."

"And so do you."

Another lecture she didn't want to hear. "I'm perfectly happy with my life," she automatically said, then veered her sister onto a different topic before she had a chance to call her on that particular fib. "You wanted to talk to me about Christmas?"

"Oh, yeah. Marc and I were thinking about spending the holiday in Tahoe skiing. I wanted to make sure you were okay with that."

An odd pressure constricted Jessica's chest, and she managed, just barely, to keep her voice steady. "Why wouldn't I be okay with that?"

"Because you'd be spending Christmas without me."

For the first time ever. Every other year she and Brooke flew out to West Virginia to spend the holiday with their mother and stepfather, but this was the year they stayed in Denver—and she usually accompanied Brooke to the Jamisons' for their family get-together.

Jessica didn't miss the tinge of guilt and reluctance lacing Brooke's voice, and knew her sister would cancel her trip if she suspected that Jessica felt even a glimmer of longing to spend the holiday with her. Jessica didn't begrudge Brooke the time alone with her husband, and she wasn't about to spoil her sister's plans.

"I'll be fine, really, Brooke," she said, keeping her tone upbeat and cheerful. "It's not a big deal."

Brooke hesitated for a moment. "Well, I think you ought to consider stopping by Marc's parents' on Christmas. I know Kathleen would love to see you."

Jessica couldn't help but shake her head at her sister's protective nature. As much as she knew the Jamisons would welcome her for the holiday, it just wouldn't be the same without Brooke there. Yet, to appease her sister, she said, "I'll think about it."

"Good." Brooke sounded satisfied with that. "Now, back to New Year's Eve. How about you and I pick a day before Christmas to go to lunch and go shopping together for dresses for the party?"

Her sister's enthusiasm brought a smile to her lips. "I'd like that."

"Me, too. Let me know when is good for you, and I'll take the day off work. We'll have a girls-only outing."

They said their goodbyes, and Jessica hung up the phone. And suddenly, inexplicably, she felt very much alone...and not so perfectly happy with her solitary life.

"I FOUND A CATERER who's available for our New Year's Eve party, and they faxed me a menu of appetizers, along with the cost." Jessica slid the estimate toward Ryan, who was sitting next to her at his kitchen table. "What do you think?"

He picked up the piece of paper and considered the items in a very businesslike manner. She'd been at his house for half an hour, and so far, his behavior had been nothing short of exemplary. He hadn't issued even one sexual advance or flirtatious overture, nor had he mentioned anything of what had transpired between them the last time they'd been together. He hadn't even discussed his request for her to think about accompanying him to his firm's party. There were no casual touches, or heated glances. Indeed, judging by his pragmatic expression, he could have been dealing with one of his clients.

She told herself she was glad he was being efficient and agreeable—it made planning the party so much smoother, and kept their relationship on a more even keel. Yet his passive attitude actually bothered her. She was used to bantering with Ryan, and fending off his sexy, suggestive taunts. Though her body was still very much aware of him sitting next to her, he appeared unaffected by her presence.

She found his polite pleasantry, well, *frustrating*.

Now that he'd had time to mull over her last rejection, had he decided that she just wasn't worth pursuing? Maintaining a purely friendly relationship would be for the best, of course, and exactly what she wanted, she reminded herself.

Or did she?

She wasn't sure anymore. While she knew Ryan couldn't provide her with the happily-ever-after she wanted for herself, there was one blatant fact she couldn't refute: Ryan Matthews was the sexiest man she'd ever met, and she wanted him.

Sneaking a glance at him as he bent his head over the caterer's list, she took in his strong profile, the chiseled line of his jaw, and those firm lips that had shown her sinful delights. She blamed Ryan for introducing her to such carnal pleasures and filling her head with lascivious thoughts. She held him responsible for making her imagine night after night what it would be like to indulge in a slippery, sensual, erotic interlude with him and sample the sweet, heady, euphoric taste of sex.

He set the list back on the table and met her gaze. His eyes were dark brown and warm, but lacked the teasing sparkle she was used to seeing. "I'm impressed. There's quite a selection to choose from."

Having been taught a very memorable lesson on the effects of diversity, she'd made sure they had a wide variety at their disposal. "I thought we could get a vegetable tray, along with a meat and cheese tray, and rolls and condiments," she said. "Then we can each choose three different appetizers, and that should make a nice assortment for everyone to snack on."

"Fair enough." He rubbed his hand along his jaw, and consulted the list again. "I'll go with the chicken fingers, fried mushrooms, and crab rangoon."

She jotted down his selections in her notebook to relay to the caterer next week. "And I'll pick the antipasto salad, mini quiches, and pizza rolls."

He passed her the appetizer list and grinned in that easy-going manner he'd seemingly adopted for the day. "Sounds great."

They spent the next hour companionably, discussing other aspects of the party. She went over her ideas for New Year's Eve party favors, and without argument Ryan agreed with her vision. He helped her decide on the drinks and types of alcohol they'd serve, and didn't reject her decorating plans to transform his home with evergreen, twinkling lights, floral arrangements and scented candles.

All in all, they settled the planning with minimum fuss.

As she bent her head over her notepad, she felt something rub up against her calf. For a moment she thought it was Ryan's leg, until a soft, plaintive meow caught her attention. Setting her pen on the table, she glanced down to find a fluffy gray cat sitting on the tiled floor between her and Ryan.

Jessica smiled, charmed by the big green eyes staring up at her. "Well, hello there."

Another dainty meow in response.

Ryan gently scooped up the feline and settled her onto his jean-clad lap. "I don't believe the two of you met the last time you were here. This is my housemate, Camelot."

Jessica watched Ryan's long fingers stroke along Camelot's spine. The cat's eyes drooped slumberously, and a contented purr rumbled in her throat. A shiver coursed through Jessica. She knew exactly how the feline felt, because Ryan had the same effect on her when he touched her.

Which he hadn't done all afternoon.

She scratched Camelot under her chin, and the cat

stretched her neck out for better access. "She's a beauty."

"And a bed hog," Ryan added, humor in his deep voice. "It doesn't matter that I have a king-sized mattress. Wherever I sleep is exactly where she wants to curl up—usually right between my feet so I can't move without jostling her."

Jessica laughed, though she couldn't help but envy the cat for having the luxury of sleeping with such a sexy man. Before her thoughts took a decidedly provocative turn, with *her* starring as Ryan's bedmate, she focused her mind back on business. "By the way, I spoke with Brooke, and she said that she and Marc will be at the party."

"And Marc left a RSVP message on my recorder, too, which is a good thing." He grinned, and continued petting Camelot, who'd gone on to lovingly knead his thigh with her paws, her adoration of her owner obvious. "We couldn't have the party without them."

She nodded, realizing their luck in that area. "Though I'm sure we would have figured out some way to persuade them to be here." She glanced over the party's agenda. "So, you're okay with everything we decided on today?"

He shrugged as if it were all of little consequence to him. "Sure."

Amazing how quickly they wrapped things up when she had his cooperation. She gathered her papers and organized them into a neat pile, unable to believe that Ryan was going to let her leave without attempting to waylay her. She should have been grateful for his courteous, accommodating conduct, but she found herself undeniably disappointed instead.

"You're making this way too easy on me, Matthews," she commented lightly. And now that they had the details nailed, there wasn't any reason for her to spend extra time with him.

"I think you learned your lesson about giving up safe and practical for variety. As well as the value of compromising."

She stuffed her party planning notes into her tote bag and glanced his way, seeing a glimmer of the Ryan she was used to dealing with in the teasing tone of his voice. "Okay, I knew this was coming," she said, reading a deeper meaning into his comment. "You're gloating."

"I am not," he replied evenly, still maintaining that relaxed, blasé composure.

His expression was completely impassive, but she was beginning to read Ryan well enough to suspect he was feeling too confident inside. "Are too."

His long fingers burrowed into Camelot's soft fur as he rubbed her back, and he tipped his head inquisitively at Jessica. "What do you think I'm gloating over?"

As if he didn't know. "The fact that you proved me wrong about the cakes."

His shoulder lifted in a casual shrug, and the corner of his mouth eased into a sexy grin. "I thought it was a lesson well learned."

A lesson in seduction. Heat and desire curled through her, and she fought valiantly to shake the sensation.

"And speaking of lessons," he continued in a deep drawl. "There is one more thing I want to discuss with you before you leave."

She sent him a curious glance. "What's that?"

"Have you bought your gift for Brooke and Marc yet?"

She capped her pen and dropped it into her purse. "I picked up a few of those extra-big bath towels at a sale yesterday, but I still need to find the other items I wanted to get them."

He worked his jaw as he thought about that for a few seconds. "Are you still intent on buying your own gift for them, instead of going in together on our individual ideas?"

She sighed. So, they were back to that issue. "Yes. I still believe that my gift idea is more—"

"Practical and sensible," he finished for her, his tone indicating what he thought of her way of thinking—*boring.*

She straightened defensively. "It's what *I'd* want for a gift."

A dark brow lifted. "Really?"

The challenge lacing his voice and the glimmer of deviltry in his gaze sparked something deep within her...an illicit excitement and forbidden thrill. "Yes, *really.*"

He blinked lazily, and resumed lavishing attention on Camelot. "Have you ever sat in a big bathtub with a man?"

She tucked a swath of hair behind her ear, hating that her answer would show too much of her inexperience. "No."

"Then you have no idea what it feels like to have your back scrubbed, or to have someone else soap up your body, slowly, leisurely..."

She resisted the urge to squirm in her chair. The mesmerizing huskiness of his voice and his calculated words caressed her, finding and touching all those secret warm places of hers. She watched his big hands stroke over the cat, and desire and need tightened her belly.

With effort, she flashed him a sassy grin. "My loofah works just fine, thank you very much."

He chuckled softly. The sound wrapped around her, as intimate as an embrace. Suddenly, everything about him had taken on sexual overtones.

"But it's not nearly as much fun as two slick bodies sliding against each other," he murmured. "And then there are the body paints I was telling you about, and the silky feel of fingers gliding over sleek skin as you draw funny, sexy pictures on your lover's back, then lick them off."

Her pulse skittered wildly at the image that popped into her mind. Now *this* was the Ryan she knew, taunting and teasing her with words. He wasn't physically touching her, but his words had a powerful effect on her body.

She glanced away from his direct stare, but her feminine nerves continued to tingle with awareness. "I'll have to take your word for it."

He nudged Camelot off his lap, and the feline jumped down and sauntered over to her food bowl. Ryan scooted back his chair, stretched out his long, muscular legs, and folded his hands over his flat stomach. "If you have no idea what any of that is like, how can you be so sure that you'd prefer towels and a hamper and a vanity set over more sensual pleasures?"

Indeed. His question was legitimately inquisitive, and she wished she had a better answer for him than the one that fell from her lips. "I suppose I shouldn't knock it until I've tried it, but what can I say? I *am* practical, always have been." And she suddenly wondered what she'd missed as a result of having grown up being so careful and prudent.

Slippery, sensual, erotic sex.

"And you're too damn proud of that fact." There was no criticism in his tone, just warm amusement. Standing, he held out his hand to her. "Come on, Jessie, I want to show you something."

Not budging, she eyed his outstretched hand dubiously. "Said the spider to the fly."

He laughed. "But you're curious, aren't you?"

Oh, more than he could ever know. She was tempted beyond reason, and she struggled to hold tight to her more reserved nature. "Why can't you just tell me what it is?"

"Because it would be much more fun to *show* you." He waggled his fingers, enticing her. "You can either take my hand, Jessie, or you can leave. It's *your* choice and I'll go with whatever you decide. But if I know you, it'll drive you nuts all the way home, thinking about what I wanted to show you, wondering what I had in mind..."

A tiny shiver rippled through her. He *did* know her. And it would drive her crazy not knowing where he'd planned to lead her. While her heart told her to bolt for the door and put as much distance as she could between her and Ryan, her traitorous body tended to gravitate toward the promises in his gaze.

Telling herself she only meant to appease her interest and would only spare a brief glimpse at his surprise, she stood and placed her hand in his. Immediate warmth engulfed her as he entwined their fingers. Without hesitating, she allowed him to guide her up the spiral staircase and into his master bedroom. She caught a quick hint of bold, masculine colors of hunter green and navy blue, and dark oak furniture, before he tugged her closer to the king-sized bed and the big basket sitting in the center nearly overflowing with ingredients of a sensual variety.

She took quick inventory of the items, finding bottles of bath products, candles, a bottle of wine with two crystal glasses, and a rich, purple, velvet chenille robe tucked to the side. There was more, but she'd seen enough to catch the gist of Ryan's gift.

"Okay, I get the idea," she said, meeting his warm, chocolate-brown gaze. "But I still think Brooke and Marc will find my gift more useful."

"This isn't for them. This is lesson number two." He released her hand, and grinned wickedly. "My sensual versus your practical."

It took a moment for his meaning to sink in, but when it did, her eyes widened incredulously. "You want *me* to take a bath with *you*?"

"In a matter of speaking, yes." He spoke as though his suggestion was nothing out of the ordinary. "Since you're so skeptical about my gift idea, I thought we'd give practical application a try to convince you otherwise."

Too easily, she recalled his cake test, and his creative, provocative way of convincing her that variety was a very good thing. Just remembering what had transpired in her kitchen, on her table, made her feel weak in the knees, breathless, and flushed with shameless anticipation.

She shoved those thoughts from her head. "Ryan, what you're suggesting is..."

"Tempting?"

Oh, yeah. Knowing the state of ecstasy he could so

easily bring her to, she was definitely inspired to accept his invitation. "How about *outrageous?*"

"Aw, come on, Jessie," he cajoled. "Since you've never had this particular experience, I want to show you how fun sharing a bath with someone can be. Then you might have a better appreciation for my gift."

A deep fluttering stirred in her belly, and she shook her head adamantly. "I'm *not* getting naked with you."

"Yeah, I kinda figured that was too much to hope for." A mischievous light twinkled in his eyes. "So, we switch to Plan B."

Her gaze narrowed. "Which is?"

"You leave your underwear on," he said matter-of-factly.

Abrupt laughter escaped her, full of humor. "How about Plan C, *no way?*"

He propped his hands on his hips, looking too persuasive, and way too male. "It's not a big deal, Jessie. It'll be just like you're wearing a bathing suit. And I'll wear my swim trunks. I promise you'll keep your underwear on the entire time, and if things go too far for you, all you have to do is tell me to stop, and I swear I will."

She bit her bottom lip indecisively. His brown eyes were honest and sincere, reminding her that he'd never taken advantage of her. Admittedly, she'd always been a willing participant in his various seductions.

And that's what worried her. Wearing her bra and panties and being submersed in a tub full of water might keep her safe from his gaze, but she had little defense against the other more lethal weapons he had at his disposal, like his drugging kisses, his insidious touch, his arousing words...

"Tell you what," he said, catering to her hesitancy.

"If after I'm done you still feel that my gift idea doesn't have merit, I'll go in on your gift without complaint or further argument. But you can't say no to me until you at least give my idea a try. Fair enough?"

She smirked. "Does a lawyer know the meaning of fair?"

He stared at her for a long moment, looking as though he wanted to debate her distrustful comment. Then, seemingly deciding if he did so he'd risk losing her cooperation, he let it go. "How about just for a little while we forget about my profession, and reduce this to something more simplistic and basic, like a man and a woman having a little fun together. Can you do that for the sake of our experiment?"

This was it, no more hedging. Say yes and treat herself to whatever pleasures Ryan had in store, or choose no and regret losing out on the unique experience he'd offered.

Her pulse raced wildly, and her answer rushed forward, based purely on the intense need and passion clamoring within her. "Yeah, I can do that."

His smile was relieved. "Good."

She watched him head toward his dresser drawers and retrieve a pair of swim trunks. Then he pulled off his sweatshirt and tossed it on the bed. Her mouth went dry at the sight of the wide expanse of his chest, muscled and defined with a light sprinkling of ebony hair that whorled around his dark, flat nipples, then spread downward, around his navel, then on to the waistband of his jeans...where his fingers were busy releasing the snap.

Her heart lodged in her throat. "What are you doing?" she blurted.

He lifted his head and sent her a peculiar look. "Getting undressed. I suggest you do the same."

Without an ounce of decorum, he unzipped his jeans and she watched in fascination as the front placket spread open, revealing a glimpse of white cotton and other masculine assets. Before he could completely shuck his pants and briefs, she came to her senses.

"Well, if you don't mind, I'd like some privacy in which to strip down to my underwear." Ridiculous or not, she wasn't used to prancing around in front of a man in her bra and panties.

A wry grin canted his mouth, as if he found her request incongruous, considering he'd eventually see her in her bare essentials. "As you wish." Withdrawing the chenille robe from the basket, he dropped it on the bed. "I guess I'll leave this for you—for *modesty's* sake."

"Thank you." She made a face at him that lightened the moment and made him laugh.

Grabbing his swim trunks and the basket of goodies, he headed toward the bathroom, then stopped short of crossing the threshold. "Just come on in when you're ready."

The door closed behind him, leaving Jessica to wonder if she'd ever truly be ready for Ryan Matthews.

6

JESSICA TOED OFF her sneakers and pulled off her socks,
then froze when she heard the water in the bathroom
turn on and rush to fill the tub. Her pulse skittered erratically at the thought of sharing that bath with Ryan,
and her gaze darted to the bedroom door. It wasn't too
late to bolt and get the heck out of there.

That would be the smart, logical thing to do. But she
could no longer deny desires that had lain dormant for
years—wants and needs that came alive around Ryan.
Whatever he had planned with this particular lesson,
she wanted to indulge her senses, wanted to play and
have fun with him.

She expected touching, obviously, and maybe some
kissing. Drawing on his chest with edible body paints
and licking it off didn't sound half bad, either. All pleasurable stuff.

His sensual versus her practical.

Deciding the experience could prove to be a very illuminating one, she reached for the hem of her over-
sized sweatshirt and drew it over her head. After fold-
ing that article of clothing neatly and placing it on the
bed, she slipped her fingers into the waistband of her
baggy sweatpants and shimmied them down her legs
and off. She reached for the robe Ryan had left for her,
and stopped short when she caught a glimpse of her
reflection in the mirror over his dresser.

Seeing herself through different eyes, she grimaced at how plain and uninspiring her choice of lingerie was. There was absolutely nothing sexy or tantalizing about her underwear, and nothing to stimulate lust in a man. Her bra was ordinary and comfortable, without a hint of lace to scallop over the fullness of her breasts, and her panties were plain ol' cotton Jockeys for women.

A sex kitten she was not. She never spent her money frivolously, and sexy lingerie was a luxury she'd never been able to justify for herself. But, it was for the best. At least her unflattering attire would help to diffuse Ryan's interest, and make it easier for her to pretend that she really was wearing an unimpressive white bikini.

Still feeling an initial twinge of modesty, she shrugged into the robe, and luxuriated in being swallowed up by soft, warm layers of chenille. Tying the sash, she headed toward the bathroom, knocked lightly to let Ryan know she was entering, then opened the door—and was instantly greeted by the delectable scent of ripe, sweet strawberries swirling from the steamed water in the tub.

Except Ryan's tub wasn't your standard fare—it was like a miniature Jacuzzi, large enough to seat more than two, and deep enough to immerse yourself up to the shoulders. Water eddied from jets situated along the rounded contour of the tub. And if that lavishness wasn't enough to throw her for a loop, then the way Ryan had transformed the bathroom into a palace of sin and seduction certainly did.

The basket of bath products sat on a ledge behind the tub, along with the open bottle of wine, and two full crystal glasses. Half a dozen candles flickered in the room, adding to the romantic atmosphere, and the fragrant scent of lush strawberries saturated her senses—all designed to influence her into agreeing to his gift idea.

"So, what do you think?" Ryan asked from behind her.

She turned and met his gaze, thinking he was on his way to contradicting her sensible nature with yet another valuable lesson—this one on the benefits of being amorous and innovative.

"I'm very impressed." With the sensual display he'd painstakingly arranged, and the magnificent, athletically built body he possessed. Wearing nothing but a pair of navy swim trunks, he was all male, virile and breathtakingly dynamic.

"That's a good start," he said, moving closer to the tub, and her. "Now off with the robe and into the water."

As nonchalantly as possible, and with a confidence that belied the anxiety thrumming through her blood, she untied the sash and let the chenille slip from her shoulders. The material pooled to the floor around her feet, baring herself to Ryan's gaze, which she felt as scorching as a brand.

"Oh, man," he groaned, the anguished sound rumbling deep in his throat.

Self-consciousness swept over her, until she looked at him, saw the pained look on his face, and found its cause in the erection straining the front of his trunks. His gaze traveled down her slender form, lingering on her bra, skimming to her panties, then taking in the length of her legs in a slow, leisurely journey.

Heat and awareness prickled her skin. "You said it would be like me wearing a swimsuit," she said, unable to help the slight accusatory note in her voice. At the moment, she felt as if she were completely naked.

His expression turned adorably sheepish. "Well, it is...kind of."

"Kind of?" She lifted a brow and lowered her gaze to his arousal. "Do you have that kind of reaction to other women you see in bathing suits?"

He grinned unrepentantly. "Not exactly." He pushed his fingers through his thick hair and drew a deep breath. "You see, my *brain* knows that what you're wearing is equivalent to a swimsuit, but my *eyes* are finally seeing the incredible body you hide beneath loose, baggy clothing, and my hormones take over from there. I always knew you'd have gorgeous breasts and great legs, but my fantasies didn't do you justice. In reality, you're so much more perfect, in every way."

She felt her body flush from head to toe from his compliment, and his direct, candid stare caused her heart to flutter in her chest. The man was a rogue, a flirt—she knew that, but she wasn't immune to his flattery. She'd never been appraised so openly, had never felt so desirable and sexy, despite the no-nonsense cotton underwear she wore.

It was a novel experience for her to feel so attractive. All her life she'd been cautious with the opposite sex and extremely reserved, having learned through her mother's experience with her father, along with her sister's first marriage, that men weren't always what they seemed. Her brief relationship three years ago supported that theory, as well.

She'd applied the same philosophy to Ryan, more so because of his profession. His career alone, his ambition and drive, identified him as the type of guy she ought to avoid at all costs. By his own admittance he preferred short-term relationships, which went against her more traditional values.

But the man...he was kind, and caring, and sincere, a direct contradiction to what his profession implied and what she'd always believed. He had a way of weakening her defenses, and tapping into intimate longings she could no longer suppress.

Unable to sort out all the confusion in her mind at the moment, she focused on the one thing that was clear-cut and undeniable—her attraction to Ryan. It was an incredibly heady experience to know that she starred in his fantasies, and for today, she was going to enjoy his attention and interest without expectations or promises.

He tipped his head, causing a lock of dark hair to fall over his forehead. "Ladies first," he said, waving a hand toward the tub.

She climbed into the bubbling, churning water, and sank into its depths. She groaned as her entire body softened, lulled by the silky heat of the water, the jets pulsating gently against her muscles, and the intoxicating scent of strawberries.

"You like?" Ryan asked as he settled himself at the opposite end. Their legs tangled as they both tried to find a comfortable position, their skin slick from whatever bath product he'd put in the tub.

She rested her head against the rim, uncaring that the hair brushing her shoulders was getting wet. "Oh, I definitely like. This is *wonderful*."

"I'm glad you approve." He handed her one of the glasses of wine, and took the other for himself. "But it gets better than this."

"Impossible," she said with a smile. She took a deep

drink of the pale pink liquid, and wasn't surprised to find it flavored with a hint of strawberry, too.

He winked at her, then reached for something within the basket. "You just close your eyes, relax, and let me show you how good it gets."

Taking another quick sip of her wine, she set the half-empty glass on the ledge, then did as he instructed, allowing her sumptuous surroundings to draw her into a blissful state of tranquility...until she felt Ryan's fingers curl around her ankle.

She tensed at first, then grew pliant once again as he began washing her with a silky, soapy sponge. He spent an inordinate amount of time on her legs, tickling her feet playfully until she laughed and begged him to stop, then moved on to find an erogenous zone behind her knee that made her gasp and squirm. The sponge glided upward along her thighs, dipping between them, but he didn't stroke her intimately as she expected. In fact, it seemed as though he was deliberately avoiding doing that.

Water sloshed in the tub and lapped around her shoulders as he shifted his position and moved closer. He continued to pamper her, gently scrubbing her belly, then past her heavy, sensitive breasts to her chest, her collarbone, and her arms. Although he'd diligently evaded all the places that ached for his touch, he'd managed to arouse her to a breathless pitch of need.

"There's nothing like good clean fun, huh?"

She shivered at the husky timbre of his voice, and blinked her lashes open, meeting his dark brown gaze that told her he was just as affected as she was. She smiled, and made a grab for the sponge, which he relinquished with ease.

"I think it's my turn to get *you* clean," she said, anticipating the task. Sitting up on her knees for leverage, she lathered the sponge with the fragrant soap and returned the favor of scrubbing his sleek, muscled skin. She reveled in the sight and feel of the taut cords of muscles across his chest, down his belly, and along his thighs. His flesh was smooth and slick from the water and soap, and when she moved behind him, she couldn't resist running her fingertips along his perfectly sculpted back.

A shudder coursed through him, and his breathing grew shallow...the only indication that he was affected at all by her ministrations. A private, satisfied smile curved her mouth. Emboldened by a sexual confidence unfamiliar to her, and wanting to see how far he'd allow her to go, she cruised her flattened palms along his lean sides, and stole around to his chest. Her fingers stroked slowly, provocatively, over his erect nipples, and awareness sizzled. She rubbed her breasts against his back, and widened her thighs to slip closer.

His body tensed, and she closed her eyes and grew bolder. Her splayed hands roamed south, and then her fingertips grazed his fierce erection beneath the fabric of his swim trunks. With a low, vivid curse, he grabbed her wrists and turned around, nearly pulling her under the water with his abrupt move. He caught her just in time with one hand behind her back and the other grasping her bottom, and she instinctively curled her legs around his to keep her from sliding lower. She gasped as their bodies came into direct, intimate contact.

His gaze darkened, but the gold around his irises glittered with the bright flame of desire. "I think you're enjoying yourself a little too much," he murmured.

She flashed him a sassy smile while attempting to regain her equilibrium. "Wasn't that the purpose of your lesson?"

He helped her back to a sitting position, then reached into the basket and rummaged through the contents. "Yeah, I suppose it was, so pay attention."

She tried to look around him to see what he was doing, but his broad, bare shoulders provided a much more interesting distraction. "Pay attention to what?"

Producing a jar of body paint, he waggled his brows at her. "The *real* fun is about to begin." Opening the plastic container, he dipped his index finger into the thick brown substance and took a tentative sample.

Curious, she asked, "Does it taste good?"

He extended the jar toward her, a subtle, sexy challenge in his eyes. "See for yourself."

She coated her finger with the flavored body paint, but instead of licking off the delicacy, she gave in to the reckless impulse to smear the sticky syrup along his chest, then leaned forward to lap it off with her tongue. "Ummm, it tastes like chocolate." Feeling daring and naughty, she nibbled a little more, letting her teeth graze his firm flesh, his taut nipple.

Seemingly surprised by her brazen move, he sucked in a quick breath. "Hey."

Lifting her head, she affected a guileless look, though she was feeling anything but innocent. "Isn't that what the body paints are for?"

A sinful grin eased up the corner of his mouth as he set the jar nearby, then moved aside the candles sitting on the ledge behind the tub. "I always knew you were a quick study."

Without warning, he grasped her hips in his large hands, lifted her out of the bath, and perched her bottom on the tiled rim. A gasp of startled surprise caught in her throat, and the immediate contrast of warm water sluicing down her body to cool air washing over her damp skin caused her breasts to tighten and her nipples to pucker...which was exactly where Ryan's gaze was riveted.

Following his line of vision, she glanced down to find that the very sensible fabric of her bra and panties clung when wet, leaving little to the imagination. Her rosy nipples were clearly outlined through the cotton material, and a darker shadow creased the V between her legs.

With effort, she managed to resist the instinctive urge to cover herself from Ryan's bold, unabashed stare, but an ingrained modesty prompted her to slide her legs primly together.

Shaking his head in a silent "no," he pressed his palms to her knees before they could touch, and gently eased her thighs apart once again. He remained in the tub, on his knees in front of her, with the water jetting around his waist.

"I'm suddenly ravenous," he murmured huskily.

The look in his eyes was as hungry and primitive as his words implied, and her pulse leapt with excitement. In slow, mesmerizing degrees, he dragged her forward, until her knees bracketed his ribs and she could feel the raw, sexual heat emanating from him.

Reaching for the jar, he scooped two fingerfuls of chocolate body paint and slashed a squiggly line down her throat and along the slope of her shoulder. His eyes lowered slumberously, his dark head bent toward her, and his lips parted for a taste.

Heart pounding in anticipation, Jessica gripped the ledge of the tub and moaned at the first silken glide of his tongue along her neck. A shiver trickled down her spine, and she all but melted at the light suction of his mouth as he savored and sampled the confection he'd smeared on her skin.

He dabbed more of the cool, slick substance down her arm, and drew swirling, lazy patterns on her skin, seemingly enjoying himself.

She laughed breathlessly, certain she'd never survive this lesson, his teasing, the torment. "Didn't your mother ever teach you not to play with your food?"

His warm chuckle was filled with wicked amusement. "Yeah, and she also taught me to eat every bite and clean my plate." Proving his claim, all five of his fingers smeared chocolate syrup along her collarbone, and he followed that with arousing sweeps of his tongue as he lapped up the mess he'd made.

Wanting to play, too, and get even with him in the process, she attempted to confiscate the jar, but instead bumped his elbow, which caused his sticky fingers to graze the upper slope of her breast.

He made a tsking sound of chastisement as he observed the dark streak of chocolate marking her. "Aw, Jessie, now look what you've done. Between the cakes and now this, you're one messy woman."

She laughed lightly. "Oh, no you don't," she said, unwilling to accept the blame for his error. "That was *your* fault, not mine."

His dark brows winged upward. "And I suppose you expect *me* to clean up the mess?" He sounded appropriately indignant, though the mischievous glimmer in his eyes gave him away.

At the thought of what that task entailed, her breasts strained against the confines of her bra, and her nipples drew into tight, hard peaks. She knew what he was asking held a deeper meaning, and his earlier vow filtered through her mind... *I promise you'll keep your underwear on the entire time, and if things go too far for you, all you have to do is tell me to stop, and I swear I will.*

She didn't want to stop. Not yet. Trusting him, and wanting to seduce him as much as he had her, she drenched two fingers in the edible body paint and traced the line of her sheer bra, and brushed across the tips of her nipples, making an even bigger mess for him to clean up. "As a matter of fact, I *insist*," she whispered, granting him the permission he sought.

Sliding her free hand into the damp hair at the back of his neck, she guided his mouth to the smudges of chocolate on her chest, and let him go to work. He took his time, lavishing attention on her neck, her throat, her shoulder, until *finally* he skimmed his lips over the slope of her breast. He found her aching nipple and through the thin material he tugged on the crest with his teeth, bit gently, then opened his mouth wide and suckled her deeply.

She whimpered as pure, jolting pleasure swamped her. His tongue swirled and laved, possessing her, and she felt that exquisite, coiling sensation all the way to that empty place deep inside her. Her back arched, and her thighs clenched tighter around his waist, wanting, needing...something that seemed just beyond her reach.

Hot, wet kisses trailed to her other breast, where he feasted just as greedily on that plump flesh and her stiff nipple, elevating her to a breathless, sensual daze. She felt his fingers, slick with the chocolate body paint, glide along her abdomen between her bra and panties, and sketch what felt like a heart. His open mouth followed the lines he drew, his tongue occasionally dipping into her navel, while his hands moved on to grasp her hips and drag her closer so that her feminine softness rubbed erotically against his chest.

Her head fell back, and her fingers tightened in his hair, needing something to hold on to. She felt wild. Out of control. Unable to help herself, she widened her legs and writhed against him, increasing the pressure building in her belly, between her legs. Sweet delirium beckoned, blazing hot and rich with promise. More than anything, she wanted to experience that mindless ecstasy no other man had ever given her.

Then his hands left her, but only for seconds. They returned with more chocolate, the tips of his fingers painting the inside of her thighs with long, luxurious strokes that made her skin quiver, and made her moan shamelessly. Then came his lips, his tongue, and his teeth as he treated her to random bites on her sensitive flesh. His nips grew sensuous and indulgent as his mouth inched closer and closer to that intimate part of her.

And then he was *there*, his fingers caressing, his breath hot and illicit. Shock, excitement, and fear all warred within her. Somehow, someway, he'd wedged his shoulders between her legs to keep them spread, and she suddenly felt extremely vulnerable in her thin, diaphanous panties, and very apprehensive of the forbidden pleasure awaiting her.

Realizing his wicked intent, she held him at bay with a fistful of his hair. "Ryan...no." Despite her protest, she didn't sound very persuasive.

He seemed to sense her indecision, her uncertainties, and attended to them. "I want to taste how sweet you are, how heady, how *euphoric*."

This is how good sex tastes.

The heaviness in her intensified, and demanded release. Witnessing the unbridled passion etching his features—the same need that trembled within her—she knew she'd forever regret this moment if she let it pass without experiencing this erotic thrill.

Relaxing her fierce grip on his thick hair, she let her hand rest at the nape of his neck, silently offering her surrender.

She expected him to strip off her underwear, but he held true to that promise and left them on. With his hands still splayed to keep her open for him, he lowered his head and nuzzled the silky flesh of her inner thigh, starting his exploration with soft, generous, damp kisses designed to make her melt. With a shuddering sigh, the tension and apprehension drained from her body, and was replaced by a decadent languor...until he turned impatient and greedy and pressed his open mouth against that feminine cove. In one purposeful, scorching stroke, he glided his tongue upward.

She inhaled sharply, and before she could recover from that electrifying sensation, he took her intimately, thoroughly, deeply. He made a mockery of the panties she wore—the strip of cotton was a flimsy barrier against Ryan's skillful methods. With slow, deliberate laps of his tongue, combined with hot, suctioning swirls, he elevated her to that acute edge of desire.

Fearing the steep fall, her fingers dug into his shoulders for support. Her mind spun dizzily as delicious abandon took over her. A pulsing, throbbing heat settled low and deep, then burst into a pleasure so erotic, so blazing, it completely consumed her. She heard him groan deep in his throat as her explosive climax hit, and then she was aware of nothing but her soft, ragged cry and the voluptuous contractions eddying through her entire body.

And in that indescribable moment, drugged by lush sensuality, she felt herself falling for Ryan Matthews, Esquire...hard and fast and incredibly deep.

Before she had a chance to recover her breath or her bearings from that incredible experience, he pulled her down into the heated water and her knees automatically straddled his lap. She only had seconds to assimilate the hard pillar of his erection pressing between them before he tangled his hand into her hair and forced her gaze to his.

His eyes were dark, his features taut with admirable restraint. His lips were damp from his intimate assault on her. "Now, I want *you* to see how good you taste." His voice was rough, sexy, and thrilling.

With his hand at the back of her head, he drew her mouth to his and shared the taste still lingering on his tongue...the sweetness, headiness, and euphoria of sex. She moaned at the eroticism of his gesture, and despite his shocking intent, his audacious words, the actual kiss he gave her was so soulful, so generous and selfless, she wanted to weep. Powerful emotions shook her, and she told herself it was just the aftereffects of the wondrous climax he'd given her. But she didn't completely believe the convenient excuse, because for as satiated as she felt physically, she felt empty deep inside, and restless in a way she'd never before experienced.

Not wanting to analyze the sentiments stealing into her heart and what they meant, she concentrated on the pleasure of Ryan's kiss. Sliding her hands along his shoulders, she wrapped her arms around his neck and pressed closer to his hard and firmly muscled body.

She shivered at the slow, lazy rhythm he set with his lips and tongue, and wondered if he made love in the same exquisite manner.

And just like that, the undeniable ache of wanting him spread through her like a reignited wildfire, from her breasts, to her belly, and settling once again between her thighs. His arousal strained against her still-sensitive flesh, and though he wasn't making any demands, wasn't asking for more than she was willing to give, she suddenly wanted to surrender to the passion and desire he'd merely shown her a glimpse of.

She knew she had no future with Ryan, just a few more weeks until the New Year's Eve party, and then they'd go their separate ways. He knew that as well. So why not enjoy the sensual delights he had to offer without any strings or promises from either one of them? Undoubtedly, the gratification would be mutual, and she'd walk away with no regrets. She'd take with her the glorious keepsake and mindless pleasure of making love to him, which would replace the memory of her one awkward encounter years ago.

Heart pounding, she lifted her lips from his, and with a soft growl of protest, he let her go, though he still held her close, making her feel safe and protected in his embrace. She moved her mouth along his jaw, toward his ear, and before she changed her mind, came to her senses, or lost her nerve, she expressed her greatest need.

"Make love to me, Ryan," she whispered.

7

JESSICA'S STUNNING and tempting invitation to make love to her reverberated through Ryan's mind like a seductive litany. Heat rushed to his groin, making him even harder than he'd already been. There wasn't anything he'd love more than to take Jessica to his bed, cover her lithe body with his, and lose himself deep, deep inside her giving warmth. But, he wasn't ready to take that next logical step, for practical reasons—he had no condoms on hand. And that was probably for the best, because he didn't think Jessica was ready either, for emotional reasons.

He craved more than an afternoon of wild, satisfying sex with this woman whom he'd come to care about, wanted more than her surrender to their physical attraction. For the first time in longer than he could remember, he didn't want a casual one-night stand...and he wanted her to demand and expect more, too.

Satiating desires was easy and simple—in the past he'd indulged in mutually pleasurable sex enough times to have affirmed that fact. But there was nothing easy or simple about Jessica, and once the high of physical gratification wore off, there would be emotional repercussions to consider.

And because of that knowledge, he needed her unconditional trust before they made love.

Her face was tucked against his neck, her labored

breathing warm across his flesh. He tried not to think about the perfect fit of their position, his throbbing arousal, and how easy it would be to give in to temptation and satisfy them both. Her body remained tense as she waited for his answer to her request.

Very gently, he eased her head back, so she was looking at him. Her skin was flushed from the steam rising off the heated water swirling around them, her expression soft and slumberous from her recent release, her blue eyes hazy. Remembering her initial reluctance to let him give her that form of carnal pleasure, and suspecting he'd been the first to do so, he had a brief urge to gloat, as she'd accused him of doing earlier.

Keeping his triumph to himself for now, he brushed silky strands of hair away from her cheek, and tenderly tucked them behind her ear. "Jessie...we can't make love. I don't have any condoms." It was the truth, as well as the gentlest way to turn down her request without wounding her feminine pride.

Surprise registered in her eyes, giving him the impression that she'd expected him to have a stash of prophylactics on hand.

He grinned, and leisurely stroked his palms up her spine to the nape of her neck, enjoying the silky, damp feel of her skin against his fingers. "Whether you believe it or not, it's been a while since I've been with a woman, and it's not as though I keep a supply in my nightstand."

A becoming blush stole across her cheeks, giving away her embarrassment. "Oh."

Finding the sponge floating on the surface of the churning water, he scooped it up and squeezed the excess liquid along her shoulders, warming her exposed skin and wiping away the smudges of chocolate that remained. She closed her eyes and sighed at the simple luxury.

"And besides, I don't think you're ready to make love."

Her lashes blinked open, and she stared at him with a combination of confusion, disbelief, and a frustration he understood too well. "How can you say that after we...after I..."

"Had such an explosive orgasm?" he supplied for her.

Obviously not used to talking about sex, she gave a jerky nod to confirm his statement.

"Yeah, your body is soft and wet and willing," he agreed, dragging the plush sponge over the swells of her breasts. "And I could slide real deep inside you right now, this very minute. But I'm not sure you're ready to make love *here*." With his index finger, he gently tapped her temple.

"In my head?" she asked incredulously. "I have to be ready for sex in my *head?*"

"Mentally, yeah. And emotionally." For once in his adult life, those things mattered to him, and he wasn't about to try and scrutinize his feelings. "I'm taking a wild shot in the dark here, but I'm guessing that your sexual experience is very limited."

She averted her gaze self-consciously. "Gee, was I *that* obvious?"

"You're very passionate, and sensual, but there's also something incredibly guileless about you when it comes to sex." Tucking his finger beneath her chin, he brought her gaze back to his. "How many lovers have you had, Jessie?"

She hesitated, then reluctantly revealed, "One. Three years ago."

"And what happened?" he prompted.

"Lane and I had been dating for about a month. I thought there was something more to the relationship, but discovered too late that he was more interested in getting me in bed. And once that happened, he decided that things were getting too serious, too fast for him, and he bailed."

And judging by the tiny crease above her brow, that relationship, no matter how brief, had left insecure scars.

She took a deep breath, and exhaled slowly. "That one sexual encounter was very unmemorable, and nothing like what you and I...well, what we just did."

He slicked the sponge down her arms, and tried not to puff his chest out too far. "I'm glad."

A look of disgust creased her features. "What, that I've only had one lover and I'm totally inexperienced?"

"No, that I was the first to give you that kind of pleasure." His hands found her hips beneath the water, and massaged the rounded curves, dipped lower and cupped her bottom. "And being inexperienced is nothing to be ashamed of. In fact, I find it refreshing, and I don't want to take advantage of the fact that you're speaking from the glow of a great orgasm when you ask me to make love to you. I don't want us being together to be a purely physical thing."

Her brows raised dubiously. "Ryan...we both know that a real relationship is impossible, that anything long-term isn't going to happen between us. So, maybe we *should* just enjoy what we know we can have, which is purely physical."

And that would make him no better than Lane. Even

if she didn't realize that, he did. Her words were flippant, a pragmatic shield to protect her heart and emotions, he suspected. And for all her talk of having a brief affair, he didn't believe that she could make love with him while keeping all her vulnerabilities intact.

And he wanted her to have no regrets when it happened.

"How can you expect me to make love to you when we haven't even had a first date yet?" He injected an appropriate amount of offense into his voice, but his grin was filled with humor. "Just what kind of guy do you think I am?"

She caressed her hands over his chest, and squeezed her knees provocatively against his hips. "A very sexy, virile kind of guy."

And that virile part of him couldn't help but rise to the occasion. He groaned, in both pain and pleasure. "So, you want to use me for the sake of fantastic sex?"

She tipped her head, her gaze clear and earnest. "Would that be so bad?"

"Yes, if your mind and body aren't in sync." A year ago, he definitely would have taken her up on her proposition. Now, he felt as though there was so much more at stake between them than just sexual gratification. It was all so new to him, this protective, possessive feeling, but he didn't want to blow this chance with her. "And until that happens, you aren't ready."

She frowned at him and flicked a stream of water onto his chest. "You are, by far, the most infuriating, dictatorial man I know."

"Coming from you, I'll take that as a compliment."

She wrinkled her nose and stuck her tongue out at him.

He chuckled. "Watch yourself, Jessie, 'cause I can

put that tongue of yours to real good use. You might not be ready to make love, but there's something to be said for enjoying foreplay." He touched her bottom lip and dipped his finger into the moisture within. "And I wouldn't mind feeling your mouth on me..."

As his very erotic meaning sank in, shock colored her guileless blue eyes and she jerked back, dislodging his touch.

"Now don't go and get modest on me again," he drawled in amusement. "I need you completely uninhibited when we do make love."

She heaved an impatient sigh, looking completely inconvenienced by his decision. "So, counselor, in your estimation, when do *you* think I'll be ready to make love?"

He resisted the urge to kiss that sassy mouth of hers, to strip off his swim trunks and her panties and take her right there and then in the bathtub.

Tucking that particular fantasy away for another time, he reined in his desires. "Oh, you'll know, honey," he said, deliberately using the endearment that definitely applied to her now, since ten minutes earlier she'd been as sweet and warm on his tongue as the name implied. "And when you're ready, you won't have to *ask* me to make love to you. It'll feel right and it'll just happen."

FROM ACROSS HIS KITCHEN table, Ryan watched Jessica reach for her second slice of the pepperoni-and-mushroom pizza he'd ordered for their dinner, take a big bite, and savor the Italian delicacy. He finished off his first piece, liking that she wasn't shy about her appetite, and had to admit that since their episode in the tub an hour earlier, a few notches in her reserve had evaporated, as well. There was a newfound confidence about her he found incredibly sexy, and it made him feel very optimistic about his decision to take time and care with Jessica before they elevated their relationship to a more sexual one.

They'd each taken separate showers after playing in the tub, to wash away the sticky chocolate from their bodies and hair. While he'd changed into gray sweatpants and shirt, she was wrapped in the warm chenille robe while her panties and bra tumbled in the dryer—which left her completely naked beneath the soft, voluminous folds of the robe.

At that tantalizing thought, a familiar heat rumbled through his veins, and he shifted in his chair to find a more comfortable position.

Jessica lifted her gaze to his, her eyes dancing with a carefree radiance that made his heart feel just as light. "Well, counselor, you're one tough attorney, I'll give you that. I think you can fairly claim victory over your most recent case."

He grinned, pleased that there weren't any kind of negative implications in her words against his profession, as there had been in past conversations. No matter how small the hurdle, her tentative acceptance was a promising start.

He tipped his head and regarded her curiously. "And which case is that?"

"*My* practical versus *your* sensual." She licked sauce from the tips of her fingers in long, languorous laps he felt all the way to his groin. "You win. *Again.*"

He narrowed his gaze, realizing she was testing her feminine wiles and deliberately enticing him with her slow, thorough attention to her fingers. He resisted the urge to demonstrate lesson number three—that if she teased a hungry tiger, he was certain to pounce and devour.

Exhaling a deep breath that did little to ease the coiling in his belly, he lifted another slice of pizza and set it on the plate in front of him. "That's because I *always* present my cases with irrefutable facts." He could see her absorbing the double meaning of his words, possibly realizing that he didn't purposely try to play the villain in any of his cases. "Utilizing indisputable evidence to the best of my ability is a sure way to win."

"So is knowing the other person's weaknesses, and using that evidence to take advantage of them."

Not an accusation, just a statement based on her own personal experience in the past. And there was just enough of a hint of vulnerability in her gaze to indicate that's exactly where her thoughts had wandered, to a childhood torn apart by the greed of her father and his attorney's quest to benefit his client.

Ryan thought carefully about his answer before replying. "Yes, some lawyers operate that way," he said, not wanting to lie to her, but neither did he want to incriminate himself. "But you can't judge all of us based on that one bad experience, not without giving me a fair chance and taking the time to gather some evidence of your own." Positive, enlightening evidence of him as just an ordinary, hardworking person, without the stigma of being an attorney.

It was a reasonable request, as well as a subtle challenge, and he was relieved and elated when she finally agreed with a quiet, "Okay."

He had no idea how they'd gotten so far off track, and he attempted to steer the subject back to a more pleasant one. "So, getting back to more important matters, is *my* gift idea for Brooke and Marc worthy of your approval?"

"Oh, most definitely." She took a drink of her soda, and dazzled him with a provocative smile. "I'll never be able to take a bath again without thinking about you sharing it with me."

Oh, yeah, he liked the sound of that. He might not be there physically every time, but he'd settle for being a part of her fantasies.

Done with her third slice of pizza, she put her napkin on her plate and pushed it aside. "You know, between the cakes, and the bath, I don't think I can take much more of you proving me wrong."

He chuckled at the wry note to her voice, but he was beginning to think that he had something else to prove, to her, and himself—that they could find some kind of common ground which they could build from, beyond their sexual attraction.

Having learned that Jessica responded more favorably to demonstrative measures, he considered his next plan of attack. Reclining in his chair, and stretching his long legs in front of him, he allowed an easygoing smile to curve his lips. "Considering how intimate we got in my bathtub, what do I have to do to change your mind about attending my firm's Christmas party next weekend?"

"Oh, you've done quite enough," she said, her voice husky with satisfaction.

He laughed at her brazen comment and the innuendo behind it.

As if suddenly realizing what she'd revealed, she ducked her head, hiding the adorable blush coloring her cheeks. "I can't believe I just said that," she muttered.

His heart squeezed with affection, along with something deeper and more intrinsic that took him off guard. He didn't try and block the sensation as he would have in the past, but instead allowed whatever emotion it was to settle in for a longer stay. "Well, I was hoping since you're still feeling content and satiated, that maybe I could get lucky, too."

A honey-blond brow rose over an eye. "Oh?"

"Yeah," he said, ignoring the faint skepticism in her tone. "Go with me to my firm's party, Jessie."

Jessica's heart pounded so hard in her chest it hurt. What Ryan was asking was not conducive to her emotions and went against everything she believed in. But then again, what she'd allowed to happen upstairs in his bathtub, what she'd asked of him afterward, and what she was beginning to feel for him now, felt so *right*, no matter how *wrong* it was.

She should have flat-out refused as she had the other night, but a deeper longing held her back, made her wish that things could be different between them.

Needing something to keep her hands busy, she stood and stacked their plates, then carried them to the sink. "Why is it so important that I go with you at all?" She told herself she was merely curious, but knew she was searching for a reason to accept his invitation, no matter how hazardous to her heart that kind of involvement could prove to be. No more dangerous than her sleeping with him, she supposed.

He stood, too, and helped her clear the table. "After our discussion the other day about your parents, and what I do for a living, I'd really like to show you a different side to the profession, that most of us are just hardworking people trying to make a decent living, trying to help our clients. There's no pressure or expectations involved here, but I'm hoping you'd come away from the party with a whole new outlook on the profession."

His reasoning was straightforward, his motivations basic, catering to her insecurities and doubts. The man definitely had a way of hitting her softest spots, and she realized she wasn't immune to his attempts.

He tossed the cardboard pizza container into the trash and parked his hip on the counter beside the sink where she was washing their dishes. "This is the first time I've ever been invited to Haywood and Irwin's Christmas party. It's a black-tie affair, quite a privilege and a boost to my career, and quite honestly, there's no one else I want to share the evening with but you."

He wanted to share the *evening* with her. How could she have forgotten that his career was his main focus, not developing a lasting relationship? Not that she was asking him for a commitment, but the reminder did help to put things back into perspective—that her time with Ryan was only temporary.

That fact gave her the perfect excuse to accept his invitation and spend that much more time with him before they parted ways. She gave her head a rueful shake—she was crazy for considering his overture, crazier still for wanting to be with him, despite every reason she had to stay away. Yet just like the situation with the cakes, just like the seduction in his bathtub, she was helpless to resist him.

She struggled between following her desires, and listening to her conscience. Done with the dishes, she turned toward him and accepted the terry towel he gave her to dry her hands, and tried to do the smart thing. "You know, I'm really not a party type of person, Ryan, and I definitely don't have anything fancy to wear to a black-tie affair—"

He pressed two fingers over her lips as a lopsided grin creased his features. "If that's the best excuse you can come up with, then it's pretty lame."

She circled his wrist, pulled his hand away from her mouth, and immediately missed the warmth he generated. "It's the truth."

"Then leave the details to me and I'll make sure you have something appropriate to wear." Before she could argue, he slipped his hands into the front opening of her robe, just below the tie, and grasped her naked hips.

She inhaled a sharp breath, shocked at his bold, unexpected move, and at the fact that she was completely exposed from the waist down. She latched on to his forearms, uncertain what he intended. "What are you doing?" she asked breathlessly.

His dark brown eyes held hers, never looking lower, while his palms and fingers measured the indentation of her waist, the curve of her hip, and the slope of her bare bottom. The earlier warmth he'd created became a raging inferno, curling low in her belly and spreading outward with every languorous stroke of his hands. Yet though she wore not a stitch of clothing, he refrained from caressing her intimately, which seemed to make the experience more sensual, more arousing, more erotic.

His fingers grazed up the sides of her thighs, causing a shiver to skip along her spine. "Size six?" he guessed, his voice a low, rich murmur.

It took her a moment to realize he was referring to her dress size. "Size eight," she clarified, and smiled. "But thanks for the boost to my self-esteem."

"You're perfectly proportioned." He blinked lazily, and dipped his finger into her navel in a very provocative way, making her stomach muscles clench in response. "And your shoe size?"

"Eight again."

"That's easy enough to remember." Withdrawing his touch, he let the folds of the robe fall together again without taking a peek at what had been so openly revealed. "Expect a package by the middle of the week."

Without his hands supporting her hips, Jessica's legs suddenly felt wobbly, and she had to lean against the counter or risk falling in a puddle at his feet.

He padded across the kitchen in his bare feet, opened a drawer, and rummaged through the contents. Finding whatever it was he was searching for, he returned and held a key out to her. "By the way, I wanted to give you this."

She stared at his offering, and knew without asking what it was—a key to his house. She kept her fingers curled around the ledge of the counter and raised her questioning gaze to his. "What do I need that for?"

"So you'll have access to the house, since you'll probably start decorating for the party next week."

She shook her head. "I'll just let you know when I plan to be here, or work it out so you're home."

"Take it, Jessie." He grabbed her wrist, and pressed the key into her palm, the metal warm from his own touch. "You never know when you might need it. And you're welcome here, *anytime*, without asking or calling beforehand."

Emotion clogged her throat as she stared into his sincere gaze. His words held a wealth of meaning, implying an exclusivity to just her, and seeking her trust. For as much as she knew she should balk and adamantly refuse the intimate gesture, she couldn't bring herself to do so, because in that moment she felt wanted and secure, and no other man had ever made her feel that way.

And even though she knew her emotions were most likely a figment of her overactive imagination, she curled her fingers around the key and held it tight.

WITH A BIG, FLUFFY TOWEL wrapped around her body after her relaxing shower, Jessica took inventory of the items laid out on her bed, which had been delivered to her apartment earlier that week with a note from Ryan in bold, masculine script stating: *I can't wait to see how gorgeous you look. I'll pick you up at 5 PM on Saturday.*

The man had impeccable taste, and an eye for what appealed to a woman's feminine side. Not only had he bought her a complete head-to-toe ensemble to wear to his firm's Christmas party, but he'd included more sensual indulgences, too. Jasmine-scented body wash had accompanied her long, hot shower, and was followed up with fragrant lotion and powder that lingered in the air around her and made her skin silky-soft to the touch.

She felt pampered and spoiled, and admitted that it was a very nice feeling having a man take care of her—a luxury she'd best not get used to, she reminded herself.

With a half hour left until Ryan arrived, she knew she had to make haste or she'd make them late for the party. Not a great impression to make on the occasion of Ryan's first invitation to his firm's elite holiday get-together. He'd obviously worked hard to earn the recognition, and the last thing she wanted to do was mar his first appearance to such an important event. The man took his professional goals seriously, and this was, undoubtedly, a major milestone in his career.

And she'd be on his arm when they walked in the door together.

Her stomach dipped at the thought. Releasing the end of the towel tucked between her breasts, she let it fall to the floor, wishing she wasn't so nervous about the evening still to come. While a part of her was anxious about rubbing elbows with all those attorneys and trying to make polite talk when she had absolutely nothing in common with any of them, she couldn't deny that she wanted to enjoy the evening with Ryan.

Determined to have a good time tonight regardless of the circumstances, she shoved those thoughts from her mind and reached for the small pile of intimate apparel Ryan had purchased for her. She selected the pair of black cotton panties cut high on the thigh and trimmed in lace, and smiled when she realized he'd taken into consideration her practical nature. As she pulled on the pretty underwear, she discovered that the combination was sexy, yet surprisingly comfortable. The translucent, stretch-lace black bra went on next, and the garment was such a perfect fit she knew he must have peeked at the label in her bra last weekend when he'd retrieved it from his dryer.

Instead of panty hose, he'd chosen sheer, shimmering black stockings with an elasticized band of lace that hugged her thighs, and when she turned to look in her mirror to see the full effect of the lingerie, she almost didn't recognize herself. A smile curved her mouth, and her pulse picked up its beat.

She'd become a sex kitten. And she liked the transformation, as well as the incredibly arousing feel of the sexy lingerie against her skin.

Finally, she slipped on the knee-length dress Ryan had bought for her, concealing the provocative undergarments. But knowing what she wore beneath the sheath of black velvet made her feel utterly feminine and decidedly risqué. The dress shaped to her curves, the sleeves were long and warm, and the neckline scalloped low enough to show a tasteful hint of cleavage.

As a whole package, with her freshly washed hair falling softly around her face, her diamond studs sparkling in her ears, and makeup lightly applied to enhance her blue eyes and features, she appeared sophisticated and elegant. All a temporary fantasy, she knew, because beneath the trappings she was just plain and sensible Jessica Newman. A woman with simple dreams of stability and security with a man, and emotional needs that didn't coincide with Ryan's future plans and his dedication to his career.

The doorbell rang, interrupting her thoughts. Quickly, she slipped her stockinged feet into the matching black velvet heels, grabbed the beaded handbag with the silk corded strap, and headed into the living room.

Giddy with the anticipation of seeing Ryan, she opened the door, saw how striking and gorgeous he looked in black-tie attire and greeted him with a breathless, "Hi."

He stepped inside her apartment, and the subtle scent of his cologne wrapped around her. "Hi, yourself," he drawled, his voice as dark and rich as the appreciation glimmering in his deep brown eyes. "You look...*stunning.*"

His warm, sincere compliment caused her heart to flutter in her chest and boosted her confidence another notch. "Thanks to you."

"Partly." Pushing back his well-cut jacket, he slid his hands into the front pockets of his trousers, and inclined his head. "I have to confess that I took Natalie with me to the boutique to help me pick out the dress, but what's beneath it was all my choice. I take it everything fit okay?"

She nodded. "Perfectly, and very comfortably, I might add."

"I tried to keep in mind your sensible attire, but you deserve pretty, feminine things, and I liked buying them for you." A wolfish grin curved his lips, and he stepped closer, tracing the scalloped edges of her bodice with a long, tapered finger. Her breasts swelled at that tantalizing caress, her nipples hardened, and he watched her body's response to his touch. "And I'd be lying if I didn't say that just imagining you in that sheer bra, those lacy panties, and those thigh-high stockings is enough to make me want to strip away your dress and look my fill."

Desire curled in her stomach, prompting a brazenness to match his mental seduction. Dampening her bottom lip with her tongue, she smoothed her hand along his lapel. "Yeah, well, maybe we can turn that particular fantasy into reality."

A dark brow winged upward, accentuating the heat blazing in his eyes. "You know, if we didn't have a very important party to attend, I'd accept that challenge."

Wanting to tempt him as much as he did her, she leaned into him and whispered huskily in his ear. "The challenge stands, counselor, all...night...long."

He groaned, the sound both agonized and aroused. "You are a *very* wicked woman, Jessie."

She'd never been wicked before, not until Ryan. He

made her feel inflamed and restless and daring, and for now, she'd luxuriate in the sensations because, too soon, she'd be alone again.

He drew a deep, steady breath, and cast a glance at the fancy black-and-gold watch strapped to his wrist. "As much as I'd like to stay and explore the endless possibilities of your intriguing invitation, we need to be on our way. Are you ready to go?"

Back to reality—his party, his world, which was so far removed from her own simple life. Reaching for her long, black wool coat, she flashed him a smile that belied the sudden apprehension infusing her veins. "Ready as I'll ever be, I suppose."

With nothing left to stall the inevitable, Jessica let Ryan escort her to his Lexus and buckled in for the ride. The half-hour drive to Phillip Haywood's estate passed quickly with Ryan keeping up a steady stream of inconsequential conversation, which she suspected was designed to put her at ease. She appreciated the gesture and thought she was going to be just fine until they started wending their way up a long, winding driveway to a huge, stately mansion. She suddenly felt as though she was way out of her league and had no business being there.

Her stomach churned with uncertainties, but she had little time to dwell on them. A valet promptly appeared to park Ryan's car, and she was forced to exit the vehicle. Ryan met up with her on the sidewalk, tucked her hand into the crook of his arm, and led her toward the enormous double doors inlaid with etched glass.

With every step, her legs felt weighed down by lead. Tension tightened every molecule in her body, and with every breath she gulped her chest burned and seemed to compress.

Oh, Lord, what was she doing?

Stopping at the front door, Ryan rang the doorbell. He glanced her way with a sexy smile, and must have seen the panic in her eyes, because concern instantly touched his features. "Hey, are you okay?"

No, I don't belong here with you. As honest as that knowledge was, she couldn't bring herself to say the words, knowing that he'd take her back home rather than force her to stay. Unwilling to ruin this night for him just so she could wallow in her own insecurities, she settled for an understated version of the truth and prayed that she'd survive the evening. "I'm just a little nervous."

He brushed his knuckles softly over her jaw, his gaze both tender and understanding. Lowering his head, he placed a quick, but infinitely sweet kiss on her lips that lingered long after he pulled back.

"I'll be right beside you the entire time," he murmured reassuringly. "You're going to be just fine, Jessie."

And then the door opened and they were greeted by a warm, friendly man that Ryan introduced to her as his boss, Phillip Haywood. As Phillip's hand engulfed hers in a warm handshake and the older man chastised Ryan for keeping such a beauty all to himself, Jessica had no choice but to trust Ryan and believe his promise that she really was going to be just fine.

8

AFTER FOUR HOURS of exchanging pleasantries and formalities with attorneys, Jessica couldn't help but let loose a little humor now that the evening was over. "How do you save a lawyer from drowning?"

Ryan glanced her way, seemingly trying to gauge her mood. "I haven't a clue," he murmured.

She allowed a tired smile to touch her lips. "Take your foot off his head."

His deep, rich chuckles filled the close confines of his car as he navigated his way back to the main road from Haywood's estate. "Thank you for saving that joke for a more private moment."

"You're welcome." The chill cloaking the inside of the vehicle stole beneath her long, wool coat and caressed her legs, making her shiver. "I don't think your bosses or colleagues would have appreciated my brand of humor quite the way you do."

He flipped on the heater, then turned to meet her eyes, visible by the illumination radiating from the dash. "Was the party that bad for you?"

With a sigh, she rested her head against the back of her seat and thought about his question. "Actually, it wasn't as bad as I imagined it would be. Everyone was friendly and warm. Any discomfort I experienced was strictly my own." And, surprisingly, it had been minimal.

She'd survived the evening, and had even enjoyed herself at times, regardless of knowing the occupation of half the guests at the party. She'd seen a different side to what she'd always believed was a hard-edged profession. The associates who worked at Haywood and Irwin were hardworking men and women who just happened to have chosen law as a career, as Ryan had suggested. People with humor and emotions. People with families of their own. People who represented the good and evil of the world because it was their sworn duty to help others and assure them of a fair trial.

But what had made the greatest impact on her was an idle, but profound comment that one of the female attorneys in the firm had made to her while Ryan had been talking to his boss. Having worked in law offices for the past twenty years, the woman found Ryan refreshing as a lawyer. According to her, Ryan was a lawyer who cared about people and catered to his client's needs, rather than focusing on his own personal gains.

And despite her bitter childhood memories, Jessica came to accept on a tentative level that not all lawyers were as cutthroat and merciless as her father's had been. Ryan certainly didn't fit the mold, and she'd been wrong for ever believing he could deliberately hurt someone with selfish intent.

"You did great, Jessie." He reached across the console and settled his hand on her leg. Though a heavy layer of wool separated her flesh from his fingers, she could feel the supportive squeeze he gave her thigh. "And I'm very glad you came with me."

She was glad, too, for purely selfish, personal reasons. Ryan had been so attentive—touching her without reserve, holding her hand, gazing at her with affection—that she'd briefly enjoyed the fantasy of being more than just his date for the evening. But just like Cinderella, by tomorrow morning the fairy tale would be over and reality would return.

She recalled the various comments revolving around her and Ryan that she'd overheard during the course of the evening. "You do realize, don't you, that your bosses and colleagues think we're an item," she said.

He transferred his gaze from the road to her. "Does that bother you?"

"Only because I'll probably never see any of them ever again, and I got the impression that they expect me to be around in the future." Which she wouldn't be, *couldn't* be.

He shrugged off her concern. "I'll handle any questions anyone might ask about our relationship."

And he'd make it clear that they weren't an item, that she'd just been a date for the evening. The pang of regret she experienced over that thought took her off guard, and she berated herself for being so foolish, for wanting something that was completely impossible with Ryan. And while she'd seen this evening that most of his colleagues juggled a career and a long-term relationship, she knew Ryan's main focus was his commitment to his career. Judging by Haywood and Irwin's enthusiasm toward their young associate, it was obvious that Ryan's goals weren't far from his reach.

You should be proud of Ryan. He's one of our up-and-coming attorneys, and has a very promising future ahead of him at Haywood and Irwin.

Phillip Haywood's praise filtered through Jessica's mind. For as much as Ryan's future goals would consume more time than a relationship or family would permit, she couldn't begrudge him the success he sought, and deserved.

Her fingers slid along the strap of her purse, and she swallowed to relieve the odd pressure that had gathered in her chest. "Your bosses think very highly of you," she said, trying to sound optimistic for him.

He grinned, appearing pleased that he'd gained Haywood's approval. "After six years with the firm, it's nice to get the recognition I worked so hard for. The next couple of years will definitely be interesting as far as advancements go."

He had his heart set on a promotion to junior partner, which was an admirable goal, as well as one that would entail more work, more hours, and no time to cultivate a strong, lasting relationship. His commitment would be to his job, and maintaining his position within the firm.

Not that that issue mattered to her, she tried to convince herself as she glanced out the side window to the twinkling lights of the city beyond the freeway. After a few minutes of silence passed, she looked back at Ryan's strong profile and summoned the courage to express a question she'd been curious about for a while now. "What made you decide to be a divorce attorney?"

Now that the interior of the car was warm, he turned down the heater. "Honestly, it wasn't *my* decision to be a divorce attorney," he replied easily. "I originally wanted to get into corporate law."

She wasn't expecting that response, and found it interesting that he'd settled for a position so different from his primary choice. "What happened?"

"Before I graduated from law school, I was hired on at Haywood and Irwin as a law clerk until I passed the bar and became an associate. The only opening they had at the time was as a divorce attorney in the family law department, and because I had bills to pay, and Haywood is such a reputable firm, I accepted the position and made the best of it." He shrugged, and cast a quick glance at her. "Honestly, now I can't imagine doing anything else."

The message he relayed with his eyes was unmistakable—he was silently asking her to accept him for who and what he was. And in that moment, she realized somewhere along the way she'd done just that. As much as his choice of career made her too aware of her turbulent childhood, she knew they'd remain friends once the New Year's Eve party was over and they went their separate ways. And despite the sudden ache near the vicinity of her heart, she knew she had no choice but to end this tentative, sensual relationship of theirs...before things became any more emotionally complicated for her.

The Lexus came to a smooth stop, and he shut off the engine, bringing her back to the present. She glanced out the window, expecting to see her complex, and was surprised to find them parked in front of his office building. The lot was empty, and the only source of illumination came from the dim lighting in the lobby.

"What are we doing here?" she asked, curious.

He unsnapped his seat belt and turned toward her. "I need to pick up a file on a case that's going to court on Monday so I can review a few things over the weekend." He hesitated a brief moment. "Do you mind?"

Of course weekend work would consume his extra time. She experienced a twinge of regret she immediately dismissed and shook her head. "No, go ahead. I'll wait here."

"I was hoping you'd come with me." Reaching out, he fingered a strand of her hair, which she was coming to realize was a source of fascination for him. "I also wanted to show you the fabulous view from my office in the evening."

Heat seeped through her veins, and a smile tugged at her lips. "Ahh, I should have known you had ulterior motives."

He chuckled, and ran his fingers along her cheek. "Yeah, I'll do just about anything to get you alone and all to myself."

Unable to resist that sexy smile of his, and what his words implied, she accompanied him up to his office, very aware of just how alone they were in the deserted building.

He turned on the overhead lights and strolled toward his desk. "Give me a few minutes to find what I need."

"Sure."

The room was pleasantly warm, and she took off her heavy coat and hung it on one of the brass hooks by the door. While he sorted through files and paperwork stacked on his desk, she drifted toward a credenza along the wall holding framed photographs.

Passing idle time, she gazed at each one, most of which were group shots. Recognizing Ryan and Natalie in one of the larger gatherings, she picked up the professional portrait to take a closer look at the older couple surrounded by six adults and five young children.

Seeing a striking resemblance between Ryan and the older man in the middle of the photo, she turned the picture toward Ryan and asked, "Is this your family?"

"Yep." Setting aside a few file folders, he shrugged

out of his jacket, hung it next to hers, and came up beside her. "There are Mom and Dad in the middle, and you know Natalie, of course," he said, then went on to point out his two older sisters by name, and their respective husbands and children.

The photo, as simple as it was, encompassed a wealth of emotion Jessica couldn't help but envy. An abundance of affection radiated from everyone's smiles, happiness shone in their eyes, and love was evident in the strength of the familial bond they shared.

A pang of longing struck near her heart, so strong it nearly stole her breath. "You're very lucky to have such a close-knit family," she said, her voice a whisper of sound in the quiet room. "Don't *ever* take that for granted."

Ryan recognized the vulnerability that etched Jessica's features and tinged her voice—he'd seen and heard that emotion with some of the women he'd represented in divorce cases. While he'd always managed to remain immune and objective with his clients because he had a job to do, he felt Jessica's pain like a vise around his heart.

Jessica was a casualty of divorce, having been deeply affected by her father's betrayal. She'd lost the stability and security of a complete family in one fell swoop, and apparently was still struggling to find what her father had carelessly ripped apart.

A family. Something he *did* take for granted because all he'd ever known was the love and support of his mom and dad, and his siblings. He'd never lacked for affection, had never gone to bed as a child feeling alone, and had never questioned either of his parents' love.

Ryan drew a deep breath, knowing it was time to

discuss her past, that in order for her to trust him as he wanted, they had to cross this hurdle together. And maybe, during the course of their conversation she could purge some of the bitterness and resentment caused by one's man lack of compassion.

"How old were you when your parents divorced?" he asked quietly.

She looked at him, initially startled by his question. "I was nine, and Brooke was thirteen." She gave the photo in her hand one last lingering glance before setting it back on the credenza. "I think the most difficult part of the divorce was that before my father left and my parents separated, everything seemed so perfect. I was definitely Daddy's girl, and I adored him. He was always so larger than life for me."

He slid his hands into the front pockets of his trousers to keep from touching her, comforting her. "I'm sure whatever problems your parents had didn't happen overnight." From his experience with clients, the strife within marriages sometimes festered for years before married couples split up—which accounted for many unpleasant divorces. He'd witnessed amicable separations, as well as vengeful ones.

"You're right, of course, and I realize now that my father must have been having an affair for quite a while before my mother found out. But as a little girl, I was so wrapped up in feeling secure, that when my dad just packed up and walked out one day, I was devastated." She shook her head, her velvet blue eyes brimming with shadows of old misery. "I just couldn't understand what went wrong, what *I* did wrong to make him leave."

Ryan balled his hands into fists, aching deep inside for the innocence she'd lost at such an early age. He imagined her at nine, carefree and filled with girlish dreams, and blinded by fantasies of happily-ever-afters, only to have them crushed by the one man she'd trusted to always be there for her.

She moved away from him and stopped in front of the huge plate-glass window overlooking the city. With the lights on in his office, though, all she could see was the reflection of herself, and the room around her. He didn't approach her, suspecting that she needed to work through this particular event in her life without interference. And so he gave her what she needed— someone to listen to her rid herself of her painful past.

"Then my father filed for divorce, and he wasn't satisfied with half of everything," she continued. "From yelling matches that I overheard between my parents, I learned that he felt he deserved everything, because he'd been the sole breadwinner. When my mother disagreed, that's when things got real ugly with my father. Come to find out, his new girlfriend was twenty-two years old and very high maintenance, and he was out to get whatever he could from the marriage at our expense."

Her shoulders lifted as she drew a deep breath, and relaxed when she exhaled, though her spine remained stiff with tension. "He hired a cutthroat divorce attorney who took advantage of my mother's emotional state and took her for everything he could, and since my mother couldn't afford a powerful lawyer, she lost just about everything to my father and his new lover.

"My mom was a mess after that ordeal," she went on, her voice hoarse. "All I can remember is her constantly crying, and staying in her bedroom with the shades drawn. It was awful, and if it wasn't for Brooke taking control and pushing my mother to snap out of her depression, I'm sure we would have ended up on welfare—or worse, Brooke and I would have gone into a foster home."

He watched a shudder wrack her slender form, and she wrapped her arms around her middle as if to hold herself together. "We moved our meager belongings from the house my mother was forced to sell, the one I grew up in, and into a one-bedroom apartment because that's all she could afford. My mother took on two jobs to support us, and because Mom was hardly ever home, Brooke pretty much raised me. We went from dining on solid, nutritious meals to eating macaroni and cheese and hot dogs because it was filling, and cheap."

"What about child support?" he asked. Surely they'd had that extra income to rely on and to help them with expenses.

She turned to look at him, and laughed, but the sound held no humor. "What about it? According to my sister, the checks came sporadically, then stopped altogether, as did my father's infrequent phone calls. I haven't seen or heard from him in over thirteen years."

She was trying so hard to remain composed and strong, when he knew beneath the surface brewed dark, bitter emotions. "It's okay to be angry, Jessie," he said softly.

"Is it okay to hate him for what he did?" Moisture glimmered in her eyes, contradicting the defiant lift of her chin. "For making a family, then walking away from it?"

"No man should ever forsake his children," he said, vehemently believing that.

Divorces happened, it was a sad fact of life. And if there was one thing he disliked about his profession, it was that the children involved were sometimes embroiled in their parents' spiteful attempts to hurt one another. He'd never given the long-term effects of that any thought while handling his cases, but was coming to realize through Jessica that the impact of a nasty divorce on a child left lifetime scars.

Compassion and an inexplicable tenderness welled within him, and it took concentrated effort to remain where he stood, when he wanted to close the distance between them. "I'm sorry that you had to go through that."

She turned back to the window. "Yeah, me, too," she said, her voice a mere whisper.

The office grew quiet and still, and little by little, understanding trickled through him, as well as a deeper insight into Jessica. After everything she'd endured as a child, was it no wonder that she'd never allowed a man to get too close emotionally?

Obviously, his profession had been the initial deterrent for her, but it wasn't the sole reason she'd built a wall of reserve. He suspected that her father's abandonment and the crass way Lane had treated her had left her feeling insecure and unable to put faith in any man's promise.

Dragging a hand through his hair, he tried focusing on the positive. "Your mother is remarried and happy, isn't she?"

She hesitated before answering. "Yeah, she is."

"And Brooke, too," he added.

She glanced over her shoulder at him, her mouth pursed with impatience. "Can you just get to the point you're trying to make with this line of questioning?"

"The point I'm trying to make," he replied very

calmly, "is that maybe it's just a matter of finding the right person."

From across the room, he could see her gaze searching his, deep and intense. "And how do you know when it's the right person?"

"You trust your instincts."

She scoffed at his simple response. "That didn't work for my mother or Brooke's first marriages."

"Then maybe you have to trust your heart." Just as he was beginning to put complete faith in his, and what he was beginning to feel for Jessica.

A glimmer of fear flashed across her features. She was scared of risking her heart again, scared of giving, and losing, and having to start all over again alone. But life, and relationships, didn't come with guarantees, and she had to trust in her emotions before she could believe in him.

Knowing there wasn't anything more he could say or do, not on the heels of this particular discussion, he turned off the overhead lights, let the blanket of twinkling lights from outside be his guide, and approached her.

He held out his hand for her to take. "Come on, sweetheart, I believe I promised you a fabulous view."

A tentative smile touched her mouth. "Yeah, you did."

Slipping her fingers into his, she followed him to the high-back chair behind his desk. He settled himself in the seat, and she didn't protest when he pulled her down to sit across his lap, then draped her legs over the armrest while his other arm curved around her back to support her.

He turned the chair to the side to make it easier for them to enjoy the diamond-studded landscape of the city and skyline. Much to his surprise and pleasure, she curled into him, placing one hand on his chest, easing the other around his neck, and rested her head on his shoulder. He could feel the warm gust of her breath against his neck, could smell the light scent of jasmine radiating from her hair and skin.

He closed his eyes briefly, and reveled in the small gesture of trust she'd given him, especially after their emotional discussion. They remained quiet, and he absently stroked the curve of her hip with his palm. Never in his life had anything felt so perfect and right as the feel of her in his arms. And never had his soul encountered such contentment as it did in this moment.

The revelation stunned him. His career and ambition had always satisfied him on a physical, intellectual level, and although he'd always enjoyed the opposite sex, he'd never needed a woman to make him feel whole and complete, had never found one who made him question the tight focus he had on his future.

Until Jessica.

He'd always known that one day he'd settle down, get married, and have a family of his own, but he'd never been in a rush to start that particular phase of his life, not with his career on the verge of taking off. He was still too uncertain of making a lifetime commitment to a woman when he knew how difficult it was to sustain a relationship under the best of circumstances.

Yet, after spending time with Jessica the past few weeks, he wasn't ready to let her go, either. What he felt for her was rare and special—he knew that, and wanted to take the time to see what developed. Without a doubt, he wanted her in his life in some capacity. He liked spending time with her. He liked the way she challenged him. And he loved how she could make him laugh at her ridiculous lawyer jokes, yet want her at the same time.

With her bottom pressed against his groin, he wanted her now. In an attempt to distract his libido, he grasped the first bit of conversation that entered his head. "Sometimes, when I'm working really late, before I go home I'll just sit here in the dark like this, just to relax and unwind."

"I can see why." She lifted her head, and smiled at him. "The view is breathtaking."

"You're breathtaking," he corrected, and ran the pad of his index finger down the slope of her nose. "But I'm glad you like the view, and that I could share it with you."

She drew lazy, swirling patterns on his chest with her finger. "It's a nice way to finish up the evening."

One he didn't want to end. Neither did she, if the wistful note to her voice was any indication. Tonight would eventually come to a close, that much was inevitable, but he wanted something more to look forward to.

He made a split-second decision. "I spoke to Marc a few days ago, and he told me that he and Brooke are going to Tahoe over the Christmas holiday."

"Yes."

"What do you plan on doing for Christmas?" He felt her stiffen against him, and suspected he'd tapped into a sensitive subject. Guessed, too, that she'd planned to spend the holiday alone.

She transferred her gaze to the panoramic view, and though it was dark in his office, the glow from the lights of the city silhouetted her profile, and gave him a shadowed glimpse of the raw emotions touching her features. "I haven't decided yet," she said, the words deliberately vague.

He knew better, and couldn't stop the tide of possessiveness that swept over him. "Well, since you have no firm plans, why don't you come with me to my parents' for Christmas Eve? My whole family is there, and it's this fun, lively sleepover."

She shook her head, making her hair shimmer around her shoulders. "Oh, I couldn't."

"Oh, you can." He grinned, and slowly glided his palm from her thigh to just beneath the swell of her breast, tantalizing and teasing her with a light brush of his thumb. "If I remember correctly, I just invited you."

She sighed as he continued to stroke along the graceful, slender line of her body. His caresses were chaste, yet aroused her, if the subtle arching of her back into his touch was any indication. "Ryan...I don't think going to your family gathering is a good idea."

The more he considered the suggestion, the more perfect it sounded. "And why not?"

"I just don't want to give your family the impression that you and I are..."

"Dating?" he supplied.

She ducked her head. "Yeah, something like that."

He heard the regret in her voice, and he didn't like it. Not one bit. "I thought we'd established that tonight was definitely a date, so technically, we *are* dating." No way was he going to let her write this night off when it had been so meaningful and insightful. "But as far as Christmas and my family go, if it relieves your mind and makes you feel better, I'll introduce you as a friend."

Interest and curiosity mingled in her gaze. "Have

you brought many female *friends* to your parents for the holidays?"

He rested his head against the back of the chair, and regarded her with a deceptively lazy smile. "You're the first since high school."

She laughed, and the husky sound filled something within him he hadn't realized was empty until that moment. Then her smile fell away, and he knew in that instant she'd realized the importance of his statement—and just how serious he was about her. He saw a flicker of panic, but before it could spread like wildfire to her brain and prompt her to retreat, he acted.

He cupped her cheek in his palm, wanting this acquiescence, wanting *her* in ways that defied his emotions. "Say yes, Jessie," he whispered.

A frown creased her brows. "If you're doing this because you feel sorry for me..."

A frustrated groan rolled up from his chest. "Good Lord, you're stubborn. I'm asking because I *want* you there, but mostly I want to share my family with you."

She bit her bottom lip, and her expression softened with gratitude, and a good dose of desire and wanting, too. She touched her fingers lightly to his mouth, their gazes locked, and something sizzled in the air between them.

A naughty twinkle entered her eyes. "Do you think you could coerce me into saying yes?" she asked huskily.

Molten heat spread through his blood, hardening him in a flash. Remembering other times he'd resorted to cajoling tactics, he knew what she was alluding to, knew what she wanted. And no way was he going to refuse her request, not when obliging her was such a pleasurable experience.

A wicked smile eased across his face. "I can certainly give it my best shot."

Delving his fingers into her soft, silky hair, he guided her mouth to his. Her lips parted on a shuddering sigh, and he took advantage, gliding his tongue deeply, touching hers, tangling seductively, stroking her in a slow, lazy rhythm. He thoroughly possessed her mouth, just as he wanted to possess her body and soul.

But that wouldn't happen tonight, he knew. With her so emotionally drained from their conversation, he refused to heap the intimacy of making love into the mixture. But also, he still didn't have any protection with him. The condoms were now at home, in his nightstand, waiting for the perfect moment, the *right* moment—when Jessica decided she wanted to take their relationship to that next level.

Accepting that he'd most likely have to resort to a cold shower when he got home, he decided to enjoy their necking and petting, and take their tantalizing foreplay as far as Jessica wanted it to go.

With a sultry moan, she shifted restlessly on his lap, turned toward him so her breasts crushed against his chest, and rubbed against him. With extreme effort, the hand he'd parked at her hip remained there, even though primitive male instinct urged him to caress and explore feminine hollows and curves.

He pulled back and looked up into her face, and from the glow of outside lights he could see the flush of passion on her skin. Her lips were damp and swollen from his kiss, her gaze slumberous, her breathing just as ragged as his own.

"Tell me yes, Jessie," he rasped. "Tell me you'll go with me to my parents' on Christmas Eve."

She shook her head and dragged her hands over his chest, finding his stiff nipples with the edge of her nails beneath his starched white shirt. "I think you need to be more persuasive."

Her lips moved up to his ear, and she traced the shell with her tongue, making him imagine her mouth and tongue elsewhere. "I *dare you* to look your fill," she said, her voice low and throaty and every bit the tease.

Her brazenness scalded his senses. He closed his eyes on a groan, recalling their sexy banter at her apartment when he'd picked her up.

The opportunity was his, and he wasn't about to refuse her audacious dare. Meeting her gaze, he reached behind her, found the tab of the zipper securing her dress, and slowly slid it down, down, down, all the way to the base of her spine. The shoulders of the gown fell off her arms, and the material draped around her waist, revealing full, perfect breasts nestled within sheer black lace, her erect nipples begging for the caress of his lips, the slow lap of his tongue.

Soon.

"Very nice," he breathed, and touched his fingers to her knee. Her eyes darkened to a smoky shade of blue, and without a hint of modesty her legs eased apart for him as he slid his palm up the inside of her thigh. The hem of her dress pooled around his wrist, and he looked down to watch the gradual unveiling of her stockings, and the lacy band that gave way to a strip of pale, soft flesh and finally a pair of black panties.

His lungs pumped hard and slow, as he concentrated on tracing the elastic band along her thigh and up to her hip, teasing her, arousing her, using pure seduction to get the answer he sought, the answer she deliberately withheld. "Well?"

She caressed a hand along his jaw, and played the game to her full advantage. "*Maybe.*"

He chuckled, liking this playful side to her, and how uninhibited she'd become with him. Very slowly, he slid each of her bra straps down her arms, until the only thing holding up the lacy cups was the tips of her rosy nipples. "You do realize, don't you, that you're forcing me to extreme measures?"

The warning only served to spark excitement in the depths of her eyes. "A man's gotta do what a man's gotta do."

He gave a tug, and the lacy webbing slipped lower, giving her perfect, lush breasts freedom. They swayed forward, her nipples tight, and he wasted no time in bending his head to taste her. She cried out as the wet heat of his mouth engulfed her, and he opened wider still to suckle her as deep as he could. His tongue swirled around her nipple, his teeth added to the sensation. She speared her fingers through his hair and sobbed—the sound rife with a combination of pleasure and sexual frustration.

He understood her discomfort, knew what she wanted, what she *needed*. And he planned to give it to her.

Severing their contact for two seconds, he turned her so she sat with her back against his chest, her bottom nestled against his rock-hard erection. Before she realized what he'd intended, he'd slipped his hands into the sides of her panties and dragged them down her legs and off, but left her stockings intact. Then he lifted her knees and draped her spread thighs over the chair's armrests.

She gasped at the wanton position he'd so easily maneuvered her into on his lap. The window in front of them was like looking into a hazy mirror, and she was all but naked except for the dress bunched around her waist, and her sexy stockings.

"Ryan?" An uncertain tremor laced her voice.

Closing his eyes to block the erotic image reflected on the window in front of him, he buried his face in her hair, and inhaled her delectable scent. "Trust me," he whispered. "And watch how responsive you are, how sensual and beautiful."

She relaxed against his chest, granting him the acquiescence he sought. Their new position freed up both his hands, and he pressed his warm palms to her breasts, kneaded the plump flesh, and groaned right along with her when she arched her back and wriggled against his throbbing groin.

Grasping every ounce of control at his disposal, and praying *he* survived this ordeal, he moved one hand gradually lower, moving over her quivering belly, up her trembling thighs, while trailing kisses along the soft flesh at the back of her neck. She continued to watch as he'd instructed, swallowing convulsively, her eyes heavy-lidded as he lazily, leisurely, built the thrill of anticipation within her.

And then, he finally touched her intimately for the first time, with absolutely nothing to hinder the feel of her slick heat and the suppleness of her softly swelled flesh against his fingertips. She was so hot, so wet, and as he eased two fingers deep within her he discovered that she was incredibly tight, as well.

The knowledge made his entire body shudder.

She whimpered as he filled her, and reached back to wind an arm around his neck, as if needing some kind of anchor to hold onto because she was on the verge of flying apart. His breathing turned harsh, and a muscle in his jaw clenched with the effort it took not to pull her to the floor and completely ravish her.

With monumental discipline, he ignored his own raging needs and concentrated on hers. He plied and stroked and escalated her to a delirious fever pitch of desire, which was right where he wanted her...on the edge of exquisite release.

She tilted her head to look up at him. Her eyes, glittering in the darkness, begged for what he withheld. "Ryan...*please*."

The hand lavishing attention to her breast plucked at her hard nipple, rolled it between his fingers until pleasure became near unbearable pain. "Tell me what I want to hear, Jessie."

This time she didn't hesitate. "*Yes.*"

Victory was sweet, and excruciating for him, but he accepted the consequences of where her dare had led. Dipping his head, he captured her mouth in a deep, hungry, rapacious kiss, as if filling her mouth with the thrust of his tongue could somehow make up for the loss of not being able to do the same within her pliant body. He increased the pressure to that exquisitely sensitive flesh between her legs, and felt her tense as her orgasm hit.

She moaned long and low as a tremor rippled through her, sweeping her up in a whirlwind of sensation. He took her as high as he could, then brought her back down with a gentleness that belied the raw, untamed fury of his own suppressed climax.

When it was over, she slumped against him, trying to regain her breath...and all he could think about was how easy it would be to unzip his pants, free his rampant erection, and enter her from behind while she sat on his lap.

Much to his relief, after a few quiet moments she slid off him and stood to straighten her outfit. Unable to watch her provocative actions, he leaned back in the chair, and slung his forearm over his eyes. The sound of her zipper echoed in his ears, and he heard the shimmy of her panties sliding up her stockings as she put them back on. His belly clenched, and his nostrils flared. Hell, he could smell the honeyed musk of her release still clinging to his fingers.

Then her soft, husky voice wreaked additional havoc with his senses. "Ryan, are you okay?"

Her guileless question almost made him laugh, but it took too much effort. No, he wasn't okay—he was certain he was going to expire from sexual frustration. "Give me a few minutes," he rasped, desperately needing time for his libido to cool.

She gave him five seconds before she touched him, and he nearly jumped out of his skin when he opened his eyes to find her kneeling in front of him and pushing his knees apart for her to fit in between. Stunned and mesmerized, he watched her skim her palms up his thighs, and gulped when her fingers worked to unbuckle the thin leather belt around his waist.

His heart drummed in his ears, and his entire body throbbed with each beat, pumping blood straight to the one organ that didn't need the extra stimulation. She unfastened his black dress slacks, lowered the zipper over the thickest, longest erection he could ever remember having, then grasped the elastic band of his briefs to lower them.

Her fingers grazed the bulge straining the confines of cotton, scorching him, setting his nerves on fire. Sucking in a quick intake of air, he grasped her wrists to stop her. "Jessie, if you so much as touch me, I'll go off."

His blatant warning didn't seem to faze her. Instead, an amused, lopsided grin tipped her lips. "Do you think you could give me maybe a minute or two to play first?"

A deep, guttural groan vibrated in his chest. "Sweetheart, you don't have to do this."

She looked up at him, her eyes shimmering with desire, and the need to know him as intimately as he'd known her. "I know I don't *have* to do this. I want to touch you, and taste you. Will you let me?"

He struggled with her request and what it would entail, not sure he could handle such an all-out assault. He was, after all, just a man—one who was hanging on to his last thin thread of control.

And then she took the decision out of his hands and put it directly into hers. *Literally*. And he was lost, unable to deny her anything, especially this.

Her nimble fingers granted him freedom and curled around his shaft snugly, measuring his breadth and length. He gritted his teeth while she explored, and squeezed his eyes shut so he didn't have to watch. Except he could feel...and when she took him into her warm, wet mouth and swirled her tongue around the swollen tip, he shook with the effort it took to restrain his natural impulse to thrust.

He swore when she deepened her intimate kiss and applied the same techniques he'd used on her... suckling sensuously, stroking rhythmically, taking time and pleasure in discovering the taste and feel of him with her fingers, her supple lips, her wicked tongue.

Heat flared. Carnal gratification beckoned. His stom-

ach muscles clenched, and knowing he was fast approaching the point of no return, he tangled his fingers
in her hair to ease her away. She stubbornly remained,
making hungry little sounds in the back of her throat
that reverberated along his shaft. Desperate, certain
this wasn't what she meant to do, he uttered a final
warning she blatantly ignored.

And then it was too late, and all he could do was surrender to her selfless offering, her inherent sensuality,
and her giving, generous heart.

9

"ARE YOU COMING?"

Startled by the question and the connotation behind it, Jessica snapped herself out of the private, erotic fantasies that had consumed her thoughts ever since her tryst with Ryan at his office five days ago. She glanced toward her sister, who was looking at her oddly.

Those sexy daydreams were going to get her into trouble, if they hadn't already. Had Brooke recognized the flush on her skin as sexual arousal, which she seemed to be in a constant state of lately? Had she made some kind of peculiar noise that had tipped her sister off to the provocative scenarios filling her head?

Jessica's heart beat triple time. Her body tingled with a desire that had yet to be fully appeased, and her face inflamed with guilt at being caught making love to Ryan in her mind—with her sister standing three feet away, her expression now concerned.

"Excuse me?" She winced as her voice came out as a high-pitched squeak.

Brooke's frown deepened. "I said, I'm going into the dressing room to try these on." She indicated the outfits hanging over both of their arms that they'd chosen for Ryan's New Year's Eve party. "Are you coming?"

"Oh," she breathed, the sound relieved. Her sister's question was completely innocent. It was *her* brain that was overloaded with sinful, lustful scenarios.

She glanced at her own selection, and knowing she wasn't in the frame of mind to continue searching through the racks in the boutique, she nodded in answer. She followed Brooke into the changing area, and they each took their own spacious rooms next to the other. Jessica hung her dresses on the hook by the door, refraining from looking into the two-way mirror because she didn't want to get lost in another fantasy, and pulled her sweatshirt over her head to change.

"You know, you've been distracted all day," Brooke said, her voice drifting over the partition separating them. "First at lunch, and now here. Is everything okay, Jess?"

"I'm fine," she said automatically, and reached for the first dress, a red sequined number that sparkled and shimmered and had a life of its own. Her assurance was meant to appease her sister, because Jessica wasn't ready to divulge the truth, that emotionally she'd been feeling mixed up and confused over Ryan Matthews. Not to mention feeling so sexually charged, she was sure her years of deprivation had finally caught up to her with a vengeance.

She wanted to make love with Ryan, and after what they'd shared at his office, she knew she was ready to take that next step. Except she'd started her period, and still had another three days to go before everything was back to normal, which meant she wouldn't be able to seduce him until after Christmas. It had been incredibly frustrating two days ago, when things had gotten hot and heavy between her and Ryan at his house and she'd had to put the brakes on any intimate foreplay. He'd been understanding, and incredibly patient, but she couldn't say the same about herself.

The thought of going all the way with Ryan was both

a scary and exciting prospect—scary because he made her feel more than any man ever had, cherished and desired. Yet despite how compatible they were, she'd witnessed his dedication to his job, in the time he spent at the office after hours handling a case, and weekend work. She knew his career would always come before her, or a relationship, and she accepted that, too. Ultimately, that knowledge kept her from doing something incredibly foolish...like depend on him. Or worse, fall in love with him. In the meantime, she was determined to indulge in everything he had to offer, because in another week and a half, their affair would be nothing more than a glorious memory for her.

"Are you *sure* you're okay?" Brooke persisted.

Ignoring the emotion knotting her throat, Jessica slipped the fancy dress on and adjusted the material over her hips. Drawing a deep breath, she summoned a light tone. "Brooke, stop worrying about me."

"You know I can't help it," her sister replied affectionately.

Jessica smiled, accepting that her sister's protective habits were ingrained since childhood, and Jessica would probably live the rest of her life with Brooke fussing over her. "Yeah, I know."

They exited the rooms to admire each other's outfits in the large, communal mirror in the dressing area. Brooke agreed with Jessica's assessment that the beads and sequins on her dress were too much for her taste, and the gold dress Brooke had selected did nothing to accentuate her figure.

They returned to their rooms for round two.

"So, what did you decide to do for Christmas?" Brooke asked.

Jessica winced. It had been too much to hope that her

sister wouldn't inquire about her plans. "Actually, I was invited to spend the holiday with a friend's family." When in reality, she'd been *coerced* into it in a very delicious, tantalizing manner.

"Oh." Brooke sounded surprised. "Anyone I know?"

Jessica closed her eyes, silently asking for forgiveness for her fib. "No, it's a friend from one of the medical offices I do transcripts for." She had no choice but to stretch the truth, because her sister would be all over her for details if she so much as suspected that something was going on between her and Ryan. And there was no sense involving Brooke when the relationship was only temporary.

They met at the mirror again, this time with Brooke wearing a leopard print dress that was too tight across the bodice and puckered at the zipper, and Jessica in a pale gray jersey that did nothing for her complexion. With a shake of both of their heads, they returned to change into their next outfits.

Jessica slipped into her next dress, a vibrant, royal-blue silky sheath that caressed her skin in a very luxurious way. She thought about Ryan, and what he'd think of the dress, and suspected he'd be more interested in finding out what she wore beneath it.

A shiver stole through her, and without thinking she asked her sister a question that had been on her mind since her discussion with Ryan in his office about relationships. "Brooke...how did you know that Marc was *the one?*"

There was a quiet pause from her sister's dressing room, then, "Why do you ask?"

"Just curious," she replied, though she knew her inquiry wasn't as simple as that. She needed to know what made a woman give her heart to a man, not that she intended to give Ryan hers, of course.

"Well, quite honestly I didn't know Marc was *the one*, not until I'd almost lost him and came to realize just how much I loved him." Brooke laughed lightly. "And it took him a while to come around, too, if you'll recall."

Jessica smiled, remembering Marc's reluctance, and his belief that Brooke was better off without him. Now, it was hard to imagine the two ever being apart. "But didn't you love Eric, too?" She had to bring up Brooke's first husband, unable to stop her own personal doubts from creeping into the conversation.

"Well, of course I did, but sometimes people don't have the same expectations of a relationship, and Eric and I realized that we married for the wrong reasons. Unfortunately, it happens sometimes, just like with Mom and Dad." There was the faint sound of material rustling and settling into place, then Brooke continued. "It's hard to explain, Jess, but I love Marc in such a way that I can't imagine living without him. When you meet the right guy, you'll just *know*."

A lump formed in Jessica's throat, one she had trouble swallowing back. She absorbed her sister's words, wondering if maybe her expectations were unrealistic. Wondering, too, if she'd ever be able to put such unconditional faith and trust in a man for her happiness, as Brooke had with Marc. The prospect made her stomach clench, and brought on a tidal wave of fears and insecurities she'd been clinging to since the day her father had turned his back on their family. She'd trusted him, believed in him, and she'd never forgiven him for callously destroying her safe, secure haven.

Brooke knocked on her door, jarring Jessica out of

her painful memories. "Hey, are you changed yet?" she asked.

"Just a sec." Pushing those disturbing thoughts from her mind, Jessica exited the dressing room and met Brooke at the mirror.

She gazed at their reflections, seeing past the outfits they wore. While she and Brooke were similar in looks, and they'd gone through the same childhood turmoil, they'd both reacted differently to the experience. Brooke made the best of situations, opting toward making responsible, sensible and pragmatic decisions. Jessica was practical, too, but had discovered it was easier, and less painful, if she safeguarded her heart and emotions.

And that explained why she was still alone and single, she knew. And she also knew and accepted that with Ryan's goals, profession and carefree outlook on relationships that he wasn't the kind of man she could have a future with, either. He'd made her no promises, and that was probably for the best, for both of them.

But that knowledge only served to make her more determined to take what Ryan was offering, and enjoy what she could of their affair.

She focused on the images of her and Brooke and the dresses they wore, both of which complemented their figures and complexions perfectly. Jessica smiled. "Well?"

"What do you think?" her sister asked at the same moment.

They both looked into the mirror, then at each other. "You look fabulous," they echoed in unison, and laughed.

"Ho, ho, ho! Merry Christmas!"

The deep, baritone voice resounded in the Matthews' spacious family room where everyone was gathered. Jessica watched in amazement and delight as Ryan's five nieces and nephews stopped whatever they were doing and turned wide-eyed to the jolly man in red standing in the doorway, wearing a full white beard, gold-rimmed glasses, and carrying a bulging, red velvet sack over his shoulder.

"It's Santa!" three-year-old Alyssa breathed, as if she couldn't quite believe her eyes.

"He's here, he's here!" Six-year-old Richie squealed in unabashed excitement.

Total chaos erupted as four little kids stampeded toward "Santa" and clamored around him for attention. Max, the youngest at two, decided to observe from a distance, his gaze narrowed, as if he wasn't quite sure who the big, boisterous stranger was, or if he wanted to approach him just yet. The adults sat back and watched, letting the little guy make the decision for himself.

Courtney, one of Ryan's older sisters, slid into the empty seat beside Jessica and spoke out of the corner of her mouth. "You'd think that Jackie would figure out that Santa is really her Uncle Ryan, but for two years now she's been just as enthralled as the other kids."

Jackie, Jessica had learned, was seven years old, and though she seemed very mature for her age, when it came to believing in St. Nick, she was just as gullible as the others. "Sometimes it's hard to let go of that illusion," she replied, knowing she was speaking from her own childhood experiences. "And it's nice to see them enjoy it for as long as possible."

Courtney agreed, and they both turned their attention back to the Christmas Eve surprise unfolding for

the little ones, none of whom had seemed to notice that
Ryan had slipped out of the room twenty minutes ago,
or that he wasn't currently present. Once "Santa"
calmed the excited kids, he addressed them one at a
time, letting each one sit on his lap and tell him what
they wanted for Christmas. Then, he pulled out a special gift for them from his velvet bag, and went on to
the next captivated child. His patience and affection for
his nieces and nephews was apparent and made Jessica experience an odd tug near the vicinity of her
heart.

Jennifer ripped open her present and gasped when
she revealed what Santa had given her, which had
been one of the things she'd just asked him for. Jessica
smothered a grin—she and Ryan had gone toy shopping a few days ago with a list from his sisters of what
the children wanted.

"Mom, Dad! Santa brought me the Herbee I asked
for!"

Jennifer cried jubilantly as she held up a small
square box for everyone to see the furry, animated
creature that spoke nonstop and was no doubt designed to drive an adult certifiably nuts.

"Thank you, Santa," Courtney said wryly, and Ryan
replied with a hearty, "Ho, ho, ho," that had the other
adults chuckling.

As Richie hopped off Santa's lap with his own gift
and Alyssa climbed on, Ryan glanced Jessica's way,
and their gazes met. His brown eyes twinkled just as
merrily as his namesake, and the wink he gave her was
very private and made her cheeks warm. Fortunately,
everyone else in the room was preoccupied and hadn't
witnessed the intimate exchange.

When they'd arrived at Ryan's parents' house four

hours ago, Nancy and Conrad Matthews had welcomed her as if she *were* part of their family, despite that Ryan had held true to his word and had introduced her simply as a friend. And though everyone had accepted his introduction without question, Jessica was fairly certain that his mother and sisters were wondering about the real scoop between her and Ryan. Knowing she'd probably never spend Christmas with his family again, she preferred that they believed his explanation.

She outright envied the love and security so evident in his family, how warm and supportive they seemed to be. They had fun together, they laughed and teased, and it was apparent that Ryan's mother took extra care in creating a holiday atmosphere meant to make lasting memories. Before Santa's arrival, the kitchen had been bustling—with finger foods and holiday treats to snack on, and with Jessica and Natalie helping the children to bake cookies to leave for St. Nick when they went to bed for the night.

The whole evening was magical and something Jessica knew she'd never forget. And for the first time since she was a little girl, she was wrapped up in the sense of belonging—and had to firmly remind herself that although Ryan had shared this holiday and his family with her, it wasn't something she'd be a part of in the future.

Jessica pulled her thoughts back to the present, and realized that all the kids had taken a turn with Santa, except for Max, who was still eyeing him warily from across the room. Wanting the little boy to share in the fun and spirit of St. Nick, she leaned forward until she caught Max's mom's attention.

"Can I take him to see Santa?" Jessica asked Lindsay.

The other woman smiled and nodded. "Go right ahead."

Jessica approached the toddler, and his big brown eyes, the same shade as his uncle's, darted from her to his mother. Lindsay must have silently reassured him somehow, because he visibly relaxed.

She squatted in front of him and gentled her voice. "You know, I've never met Santa personally, either, so what do you say we go together?"

Max swallowed and sneaked a peek at Santa, the yearning in his gaze clear. Seemingly deciding that he'd be safer with an escort, he nodded his head jerkily, and placed his tiny hand in hers.

Jessica accompanied Max to the man in red, and sat him on Ryan's knee, but remained close so the little boy didn't panic.

Santa patted Max's thigh in a gesture meant to reassure him. "I hear you've been a very good boy this year," Ryan said, his voice deliberately gruff to disguise it.

Max, eyes round as he stared at Ryan's huge white beard, nodded mutely.

"Would you like to tell me what you'd like for Christmas?"

Max shook his head "no" in response, still uncertain of this jolly, strange man.

"Well, I think I might have something in my bag that you'd like." Ryan withdrew the last gaily wrapped present, and handed it to Max.

"Thank you," the little boy whispered, then scrambled off Santa's lap and bolted for the safety of his father, Clive, who sat across the room watching the show.

Jessica stepped away to return to her seat, but a white-gloved hand caught her wrist, gently tugged her back, and she found herself sitting on Santa's very hard, muscular thigh. She gasped in surprise that he'd so openly flirt with her in front of his family when his behavior toward her had been platonic all evening.

A dark brow quirked over the rim of his ridiculous-looking spectacles. "So, has Jessica been naughty or nice this year?" he murmured, his deep, rich voice sending a shiver rippling down her spine.

She could feel a blush tingling along her skin, as well as the curious stares of his mother and sisters. Luckily, the kids were being so loud that it was impossible to hear her and Ryan's conversation.

"I've been so good that I'm probably one of the top ten names on your list." She grinned, and decided to turn the tables on him. "And what about yourself, Santa?"

He looked surprised at her direct challenge, then his eyes sparkled with a wicked, unrepentant light, and she knew trouble was heading her way. "Oh, definitely naughty. I'm expecting a lump of coal in my stocking this year, but all the fun I've had has been worth it."

She laughed, not wanting to think about the kind of "fun" Ryan might have indulged in. She was certainly well aware of how naughty he'd been with her. Feeling a little mischievous herself, she leaned close and whispered in his ear, "Naughty and nice can make for a very interesting combination."

He released a very hearty "ho, ho, ho," then added more privately, "I'll certainly keep that in mind when I bring you *your* gift."

'TWAS THE NIGHT before Christmas, and all through the house, not a creature was stirring, not even a mouse...just Ryan.

It was a quarter until midnight, the house was dark and silent, and Ryan stealthily crept upstairs, avoiding the wooden planks he'd discovered as a teenager that creaked. He snuck past his parents' closed door, and continued down the hall past his sisters' rooms, where they slept with their husbands and kids, to his old bedroom where Jessica was sleeping for the night while he took the couch downstairs. Slipping quietly into the shadowed room, he moved toward the bed.

"Ryan?" came Jessica's husky whisper.

"Yeah, it's me," he confirmed, sitting on the edge of the mattress.

"What are you doing in here?" She propped herself up on her elbow, and the moonlight filtering through the window made her tousled, honey-blond hair shimmer around her shoulders. "It's nearly midnight, and your parents are right down the hall—"

He pressed his fingers to her lips, stopping her chastisement. "Yeah, and you're gonna wake everyone up if you don't be quiet."

Her eyes widened slightly, and she pulled his hand away. "Ryan, I was just teasing about that naughty and nice thing. I mean, we can't do anything *now*, and especially not under your parents' roof."

She sounded so prim and proper, he couldn't help but grin. "Oh, I plan to take you up on your naughty and nice comment, but that's not why I'm here," he said, keeping his voice low. "I want you to come with me." He stood, and waited for her to do the same.

She frowned up at him. "Why?"

He propped his hands on his hips and exhaled a breath, summoning patience. Would she always question his motives? Would she ever believe and accept that his interest in her went beyond his original plan of seducing her?

"Because I asked," he said, deliberately vague. A simple issue of trust was at stake, and he wanted her to acknowledge that she trusted him, even on this small, insignificant issue.

After a brief hesitation, she tossed back the covers and slipped off the bed, garbed from neck to toes in a long-sleeved nightshirt, bottoms, and socks.

"Nice pajamas," he teased.

She scrunched her nose at him as her gaze took in his cotton shorts and T-shirt. "If you haven't noticed, it's winter, and flannel is warm."

"As an alternative, I suppose it suffices," he murmured. "But body heat can be just as effective."

She rolled her eyes at his innuendo, but accepted the hand he held out to her. Then, like two little kids wanting to catch Santa in action, they snuck back downstairs to the dark family room. Ryan hit a switch on the wall, and the lights on the Christmas tree came on, their twinkling colors providing a dazzling, magical atmosphere.

"What are you going to do?" Jessica asked in a hushed voice filled with amusement. "Find out which ones are your gifts and shake them?"

He chuckled. "No, you and I are going to put Santa's gifts under the tree, which has somehow become my job over the years. And then we have cookies to eat and milk to drink so the little imps upstairs will know that Santa was really here."

She glanced at the coffee table, where the kids had left a plate piled high with the sugar cookies they'd made that evening, and a glass of milk that had no doubt turned warm. A brief glimpse of melancholy flickered over her expression, but by the time she met his gaze again whatever emotional memory she'd been caught up in was gone.

She smiled at him. "Well, let's get started," she said, enthusiasm infusing her voice.

She followed him to the coat closet that doubled as a storage area under the stairs, and they spent the next half hour hauling presents out and placing them under the tree until the corner of the room was overflowing with gaily wrapped gifts. His sisters had left small bags of items to stuff in the kids' stockings, and by the time he and Jessica were done, it appeared that Santa had, indeed, paid a visit to the Matthews home.

"And now for the cookies," Jessica reminded him, caught up in the spirit of things, just as he'd intended.

After the snippets she'd revealed about her childhood, he'd suspected that it had been a long time since she'd enjoyed such frivolous fun, and it made his heart swell that he was able to share this with her. "Let me go get a fresh glass of milk."

He returned a minute later and sat beside her on the couch. The blinking lights from the tree cast pretty highlights in her hair, and made her eyes shimmer with the delight still lingering from their escapade of playing Santa's helpers.

He picked up a cookie sprinkled with red and green sugar, and popped the entire thing into his mouth and chewed. "I think this is the best part of Christmas."

She slanted him a curious look as she selected her own baked confection, then nibbled on it. "What? Eating the cookies?"

He shook his head, and washed down his bite with a drink of milk. "Knowing that the kids are going to come downstairs in the morning and see the gifts under the tree and the plate with crumbs on it, and truly believe that Santa was here." He filched another cookie, and thought about himself as a young boy on Christmas, so filled with energy and excitement, until he'd discovered the truth about St. Nick. "I remember I was so crushed when I learned there was no Santa Claus."

"How did you find out?" She shared his glass of milk, then licked the remaining droplets off her lips.

Ignoring the automatic desire that flared to life within him at Jessica's innocent gesture, he reminded himself that this weekend wasn't about the seduction they'd yet to consummate. Averting his attention, he took one of the remaining cookies between his fingers and crushed it to leave visible crumbs on the plate. "Well, I thought I'd be creative and test the Santa theory, and instead of leaving cookies for him, I insisted on making him a peanut butter and sardine sandwich."

"Oh, yuck." She blanched, her expression reflecting her disgust at the combination. "Were you trying to assure that Santa never paid another visit to your house?"

He chuckled. "Well, I remember thinking if the sandwich was gone, then there really was a Santa because he'd be so hungry from his trip around the world that he'd eat it, or feed it to Rudolph. But if it was still there in the morning, then there wasn't really a Santa, because no normal person would eat something so awful."

"Interesting theory," she said, her tone wry. "And what happened?"

"In the morning, it was gone." He licked the remnants of sugar from his fingers.

"Your parents ate it?" she asked incredulously.

"Not exactly." Grinning, he reclined against the sofa cushions and stacked his hands behind his head. "I found it in the trash. I was eight, and I think I was ready to discover the truth, but I was still crushed."

She nodded in understanding, and there was that melancholy again.

"What about you?" he asked, tugging on her pajama sleeve before she could emotionally retreat from him. "When did you discover that there wasn't really a Santa Claus?"

Sitting back, she drew her knees up on the couch and wrapped her arms around her legs. "Well, it was the year my parents divorced." She gave him a sad smile that made him ache for her. "I was nine years old, and after losing my father, believing in Santa Claus was just so important to me. A part of me knew he wasn't real, but I clung to the fairy tale."

With a soft sigh, she rested her chin on her knees and focused on the Christmas tree lights. "I remember asking for the newest, latest Barbie playhouse that was out at the time. It was really expensive, and Brooke kept giving me the spiel that Santa has a lot of kids to bring gifts to, and not all kids get what they want. She knew where the presents came from, and also knew I was in for a big letdown. Still, that was the only thing I put on my list, because I wanted so badly to believe that Santa was real, and that he'd bring me that one toy because I knew it was too expensive for my mother to afford."

She ducked her head so he couldn't see her face, but her trembling voice gave her away. "My mother was hardly ever home because she was working two jobs, and when I heard her come in on Christmas Eve after working her late shift at a restaurant, I snuck out to the living room and saw her sitting on the floor wrapping presents. And there, among a few inexpensive trinkets for me and Brooke was the Barbie playhouse I'd asked for. And in the morning, it had a tag on it that said, 'From Santa'."

Finally, she turned and looked at him, the moisture in her eyes revealing her inner pain. "As much as I loved my mother for scrimping and saving to give me my one wish, I stopped believing in a lot of things that Christmas."

Her anguish seemingly became his own, squeezing his chest tight, and the only thing he could think of was chasing away her misery and bad memories and giving her something she could cling to and depend on. Him.

"Jessie, sweetheart," he whispered, and reached for her, because mere words were inadequate to soothe her. She came into his embrace without resisting, burrowing into him like a lost soul seeking comfort. Wrapping an arm around her back and holding her close, he eased them both down onto the couch so she was lying between him and the cushions, cocooned in his warmth and strength.

She buried her face against his neck, and a great, big shuddering sigh wracked her entire body. Then, he felt the hot dampness of tears seeping through his T-shirt, and knew all he could do was just be there for her while she came to terms with the pain of her past.

He cuddled her close and watched the tree lights dance in front of them, stroking her side and hip through her flannel pajamas until her breathing grew deep and even and he knew she'd succumbed to peaceful sleep. In a few minutes, he'd wake her up and take her back to her room. In the meantime, he savored the feel of her, the jasmine scent of her hair and skin, and how perfectly she fit into his life...and he came to realize with a calm acceptance that despite not looking for love, he'd found it with her. And no matter what he had to do, he wanted to make room for her in his life, his future.

If only she'd allow him into her heart.

JESSICA SNUGGLED closer to the warm, masculine body next to hers, luxuriating in the sense of complete contentment and security enveloping her. Their sleeping quarters were cramped, but she didn't mind. Her head rested on Ryan's chest, her arm was slung over his stomach, and her legs entwined with his. A sleepy smile touched her lips when she realized that one of Ryan's hands was tangled in her hair, and his warm breath brushed across her temple.

She'd never *slept* with a man before, nor had any man ever held her so tenderly, without expecting a sexual favor in return. And despite the desire that Ryan inspired, she liked the feeling of just being held in his arms, especially after last night and the desolate memories that had swamped her. He'd silently consoled her and allayed the loneliness that had been her constant companion for far too long.

Yet, she knew the isolation and solitude would return once he was no longer a part of her life. And as much as the thought of letting Ryan go hurt, she accepted it as inevitable, knowing their lives, their aspirations and dreams for the future, didn't mesh.

Ignoring the ache in her heart, she sighed and rubbed her cheek against his chest, focusing on the present and what they had in common—their attraction, desire and passion. And for now, for today and the next week, she planned to be greedy and experience it all. And then, when that awful loneliness settled in, she'd have wondrous memories to draw on, to keep her warm on the long, solitary nights ahead.

The sound of hushed whispers and stifled giggles reached past Jessica's musings, and brought her back to the present. She blinked her eyes open and found herself staring at Ryan's three nieces, who stood in front of the couch watching them sleep. From the other room, she could hear the adults approaching, too. Not sure how to handle the situation or explain their dilemma, even though they'd done nothing wrong, she gave Ryan a firm shake.

He awoke, slowly and lazily. His slumberous gaze met hers, and a sexy smile eased up the corners of his mouth. "Morning," he murmured.

Trying not to let that husky, intimate voice of his and just how gorgeous he looked first thing in the morning distract her, she nodded toward the trio in front of them. "Uh, we've got company."

Ryan turned his head, and though his body tensed with instant awareness, his expression gave nothing away. "Morning, girls," he said cheerfully.

"Uncle Ryan," Jackie said, a slight frown marring her brows. "How come you and Jessica are sleeping on the couch?"

"Well..." His voice trailed off as he obviously tried to conjure an excuse. Taking more time, he sat up, just as the rest of the Matthews clan converged in the family room. Surprise and speculation registered across everyone's faces at seeing them together, and Jessica felt her face flush at being caught in such an embarrassing predicament.

"Hey, did you two get to see Santa last night?" Ryan's sister Lindsay asked, amusement lacing her voice.

Alyssa's eyes rounded with hope at that thought. "Did you?"

Richie dashed past his father and raced into the room, dancing around the coffee table, pointing to the plate with the crumbs on it, and the empty milk glass. "Look, Santa ate the cookies and drank the milk! Did you see him, Uncle Ryan? Did you?"

Ryan dragged a hand through his tousled hair and grinned. "The thing is, Jessica and I snuck down here last night and tried to stay awake for Santa, but we were so tired that we just didn't make it." He shook his head regretfully.

"But look at all the presents he left," Jennifer said, scrambling over to the tree and the overflow of gifts. "Here's one for me, and one for Max, and one for Grandma..."

As the kids squealed in excitement and huddled around the tree, and the adults moved in to help sort and pass out the presents to the eager children, Ryan took the opportunity to grasp a private moment with Jessica.

"I'm sorry," he whispered, appearing contrite at the awkward situation he'd put her in. "I swear I didn't mean for us to fall asleep together and wake up with an audience."

She smiled to reassure him. "It's okay."

Uncaring of who might see the affectionate gesture, he stroked his knuckles down her cheek, then tucked a wayward strand of hair behind her ear. "You ready to enjoy Christmas morning, Matthews style?"

She shivered at his touch, reveling in the warmth and tenderness in his gaze. "Yeah, I am."

And as she watched Ryan with his nieces and nephews, and was accepted so completely into the fold of his family, she knew this sense of belonging would be her most precious memory of all.

10

TONIGHT'S THE NIGHT.

Rod Stewart's raspy voice and the classic lyrics to that sexy song reached Ryan just as he stepped into his house from the garage after an unexpectedly long day at the office. Having seen Jessica's car parked out by the curb, he knew she was decorating for the New Year's Eve party, which was tomorrow night.

Using the key he'd given her, she'd spent the past two afternoons setting up chairs, bringing in party supplies, and embellishing the bottom level rooms of his house with twinkling lights and flora. They'd been so busy since Christmas, both of them preparing for the surprise party and him wrapping up loose ends on a few cases at work, that they hadn't had any private, intimate time for *them*.

Tonight, there was something different in the air, an undeniable sensuality and desire that made his blood warm in his veins and his heart beat faster. Feeling drawn in by the sultry mood of the music, and seduced by the sexy lyrics that seemed so fitting to what Ryan felt for Jessica, he headed toward the front room in search of the only woman who'd ever managed to capture a significant piece of his heart.

She'd also managed to charm his family, too, as he'd known she would. His mother had specifically called him at work to tell him how much she'd enjoyed Jessica's company, and that she hoped to see more of her in the future. Though Ryan would have liked to assure his parents that Jessica would be a part of his life, he knew he couldn't make that promise. Not yet, but maybe after tonight that would change, because he planned to take a huge risk and wear his emotions on his sleeve.

With Rod Stewart's raspy voice swirling around him, he turned the last corner into the living room, and came to an abrupt stop. Because of the music, Jessica hadn't heard him enter the house from the garage. She was busy twining a string of white lights along the bottom of the spiral staircase railing, but what captured his attention were her uninhibited, sinuous movements as she danced to the classic tune. Her husky voice sang the suggestive lyrics, while her hips swayed to the beat of the music, slow and enticing. Then she closed her eyes, lifted her arms, and undulated—a full-bodied shimmy as captivating as any exotic dancer's move.

He grew hard just watching her, wanting her with a hunger and need that superceded anything he'd ever experienced. And then it hit him...the pure rightness of the moment. Despite all he'd achieved professionally, *this* is what had been missing from his life. Jessica, with her sass and laughter and warmth. Jessica, filling his soul, his waking hours. *She* was who he wanted to come home to every day. *She* was who he wanted to sleep with at night.

And then that revelation faded as she twirled around and gasped in breathless shock to find him standing less than five feet away, watching her. Her face flushed pink, and instead of the embarrassment he'd expected, her eyes turned a dark, velvet shade of blue. The color of desire and passion.

He blinked lazily, and allowed a rakish grin to tip the corner of his mouth. "Don't stop on my account." He heard the deep, male nuances of arousal in his voice, despite his casual tone.

With a beguiling smile, she stepped into the living room, grabbed the remote for his CD player, and pressed the Repeat button to play the last song again. He thought she planned to give him another provocative show, but instead of gyrating those hips for his sole pleasure, she turned and held out her hand to him.

"I've got a better idea," she said, meeting his gaze steadily. "Why don't you join me?"

A deliberate dare, an irresistible challenge, one he was fully prepared to accept because he knew that everything that had been building and growing between them for the past year had led to this moment. Shrugging out of his sports coat and tossing it onto the couch, he closed the distance between them. He gathered her in his arms, nudged a thigh between hers, and pulled her flush against his hard length until the only thing separating them was the one inch of space between their parted lips.

But she didn't kiss him, and he didn't kiss her—though not for a lack of desire. If tonight *was* the night, it belonged to Jessica, and she'd be the one to make the physical connection between them finally happen.

She seduced him in subtle ways. To the alluring beat of the music, she teased him with the erotic brush of her body along his, tempted him with the crush of her full breasts against his chest. He followed her lead, tantalizing her with the stroke of his hands along her lithe hips, her bottom, and along the backs of her thighs encased in form-fitting black leggings.

She closed her eyes on a soft moan and moved rhythmically, sensually, against his muscular thigh. He clasped her hips tighter, dragged her closer, increasing the friction and pressure until her breathing hitched, an unmistakable sign that a climax was imminent.

The music stopped, and so did Ryan, leaving Jessica on edge and just as aroused and inflamed as he was. Her lashes fluttered open, and there it was in the depth of her eyes, the complete and total acquiescence he'd been waiting for since that afternoon in his bathtub when she'd asked him to make love to her. Now, the request wasn't necessary, because the moment was *right*, and she was ready for it to happen.

She knew it as well as he did.

Without words, she ran her palm down his arm to his hand, and entwined their fingers. Then, with Rod Stewart singing "You're In My Heart, You're In My Soul," he followed her upstairs to his bedroom. He shut the door behind them, not wanting anything to intrude on their first time together, nor did he intend to share his bed with anyone but Jessica. Camelot would have to find other lodgings for the night.

He turned on the bedside lamp, wanting to see everything...the unveiling of Jessica's supple curves, her incredible blue eyes when he finally came inside her, and her expression when he revealed just how deeply his feelings for her ran.

There wasn't a hint of modesty about her now, just a feminine confidence he'd spent the past month cultivating. His patience had been worthwhile, because he wouldn't accept anything less than her full surrender.

Easing his warm hands beneath the hem of the

sweater she wore, he slowly skimmed along her sides as he pulled the top up and over her head, then let it drop to the floor as his gaze discovered a delightful surprise...a flesh-tone, stretch-lace, low-cut bra that lifted and shaped her breasts.

He lifted a brow in teasing inquiry, boldly traced the scalloped edge of the bra that dipped into very enticing cleavage, and watched her nipples tighten for him. "What's this?"

She drew a breath that made those full, perfect mounds of flesh quiver. "I've taken a liking to pretty lingerie."

Smiling, he skimmed his finger down her abdomen, to the waistband of her leggings. "You know you turn me on in your cotton underwear, but I like the way this looks on you. And it makes me wonder what you're wearing beneath these pants." In time, he'd find out.

But first things first. Reaching behind her, he unclasped the hooks of her bra, then eased the straps off her shoulders until the lacy garment joined her sweater on the floor. Because words eluded him, he groaned to express his appreciation of what he'd revealed, then he lowered his head and *showed* her. Burying his face between her lush breasts, he inhaled her scent, then lapped his warm, wet tongue over the full slopes, grazed his teeth over the tight crests. On a startled gasp, she fisted her hands in his hair and let him taste his fill of her.

It was only the beginning. Slipping his hands into the waistband of her leggings, he dragged the stretchy fabric down her slender legs, and moved his mouth lower, too, kissing her smooth, silky belly, the insides of her thighs, and lingered there as she stepped from her pants. Then he took in the matching, lacy, beige panties she wore, and couldn't resist pressing a hot, openmouthed kiss to the satin covering her mound. She moaned, and trembled, and before he gave in to the urge to indulge in a more intimate exploration, he straightened to his full height, toed off his shoes, and pulled off his socks.

The rest was up to her.

He spread his hands in front of him. "I'm all yours, sweetheart," he said, meaning it in more ways than the obvious.

Grabbing his tie, she wrapped the strip of silk around her fist, drawing him closer. She cast him an upswept glance, full of sass and feminine wiles...and just the barest hint of vulnerability. "How can you tell if a lawyer is well hung?"

Before he could recover from his surprise at her question, she replied with, "You can't fit a finger between the rope and his neck."

His mouth quirked with amusement, but he wasn't about to let her retreat or hide behind her brand of humor. Not here and not now. "There's another way to tell if he's well hung," he said, and guided her free hand to the fierce erection straining the front of his trousers.

Dampening her bottom lip with her tongue, she squeezed the length of him, stroked him through his pants until he groaned, shuddered, and had to grab her wrist to halt her caresses.

"*Very* impressive, counselor." She tugged him closer with her grip on his tie, and settled her mouth over his, drugging him with her deep, leisurely kiss.

He let her set the pace, knowing his turn would come later. She proceeded to undress him, taking her time stripping off each article of clothing until he was completely naked. Then, starting at his neck and traveling south, she explored his hard, hot skin with the glide of her palms, her soft lips, and the wet warmth of her tongue until his breathing grew ragged, his body throbbed with need, and his control and restraint teetered on the verge of snapping. He had to stop her, or he wasn't going to last.

"Jessica..." he groaned her name, and threading his fingers through her silky hair, he drew her up against his body and slanted his mouth across hers, tasting the salty, musky essence of him on her tongue. As one kiss inevitably, enticingly melted into another, he guided them toward his bed, until the backs of her thighs met the mattress.

Reluctantly, he let her go, knowing he needed to put on protection while he was still able to think with a semblance of clarity. As she settled on the bed, and he moved away, an uncertain look passed over her features, as if she thought, *believed*, that he was leaving her. As if he ever could.

"Give me a sec," he rasped, and opened the nightstand drawer to grab a condom.

She lay back against the pillows, watching him though lashes that had fallen to half-mast. Her lips were pink and swollen, her hair tousled around her face, and her lithe body was flushed with feminine desire. She looked so incredibly inviting, so sensual, that he had a difficult time concentrating on his task.

Finally, he managed the deed, and the brief separation from Jessica gave him the reprieve he needed to continue things slowly. She smiled at him as he climbed onto the bed, and she went to remove her lacy panties—the only barrier between them—until he stopped her.

"I want to take them off," he said huskily. But first, he lavished attention on her breasts, curling his tongue along her nipples, taking her deeply into his mouth until she shivered beneath him. His lips tasted her belly, the curve of her waist, while his fingers found the waistband of her panties and slowly drew them down her slender hips, over her mound, and left them tangled around her thighs for a moment, which restricted the spread of her legs to only a few inches.

She whimpered, the sound filled with frustration. Her hand slid along his shoulder, then curled around the nape of his neck, urging him toward the very heart of her. His mouth followed the path he'd bared, the one she dictated, until her heady, aroused scent filled his every breath. A raw, primitive hunger shot straight to his groin, and he gave in to the instinctive need raging within him. Tucking his chin between her confined thighs, he delved his tongue between her softly swelled flesh and found the sensitive nub hidden within. She gasped and writhed, but he kept her hips pinned to the mattress as he stroked, suckled, and lost himself in the sweetness of her response.

Then, her climax hit. Her back arched and she cried out, loud and unabashed, and before the convulsions rippling through her ebbed, he had her panties stripped off and was kneeling between her legs, his own breathing labored. Hooking his fingers beneath her knees, he dragged her down so she lay flat on the mattress and her spread thighs draped over his, the tip of his erection teasing her glistening, slick folds.

At that moment he looked into her velvet blue gaze, and the acceptance he saw there arrested him, made his heartbeat quicken and his chest fill with a multitude of emotions that humbled him, and made him wonder, for a split second, if he could be everything Jessica needed him to be. Strong. Reliable. A man who could promise her forever.

He could be, if she *let* him.

And then the fleeting thought receded as Jessica whispered invitingly, "Come inside me, Ryan."

Unable to deny either one of them what they both wanted, he settled his body over hers until they were face to face, guided himself into the hot, liquid center of her, and filled her with one fluid thrust. She gasped sharply, and he groaned deep in his throat at the sweet, tight clenching of her body.

He'd primed her well, yet she was incredibly snug, and the erotic rush of it nearly had him unraveling. With effort, their labored breaths mingling, he moved his hips, withdrawing and surging back into her slowly, feeling her soften around him, beneath him. As she adjusted to the fit of him, her expression turned rapturous. He savored the languorous drift of her hands down his spine, the instinctive way she lifted her hips and wrapped her legs around the back of his thighs to allow him deeper still.

She'd given him her body, and there was only one other place he needed to be. In her heart.

Burying himself to the hilt in one long, smooth stroke, he stilled over her, his pulse racing erratically. He tangled his fingers into the hair at the side of her face, making sure that he had her complete and total attention. She gazed up at him, a sultry smile on her lips, her eyes hazy with passion.

"I love you, Jessica," he said, his voice unmistakably clear.

He felt her tense, saw the panic and denial that flashed across her features, and wasn't surprised at her reaction. While he'd had time to come to terms with his feelings, she'd only had a few seconds. And he didn't expect her to return the declaration, only knew that she needed to hear the words, and believe in them.

With a gentleness that belied his body's need for release, he lowered his head and kissed her, and then she *did* surprise him, opening her mouth wide beneath his and responding with a greed and urgency that shot his plan for tenderness to hell.

A sense of desperation cloaked her, made her as wild and tempestuous as a summer storm...and all he could do was ride the intense waves of pleasure consuming them both. She reached the crest with a shattering cry, and he followed, surrendering to the hot, carnal flames of his own explosive climax.

I LOVE YOU.

Curling up in the old, soft, comforting chair in her living room, Jessica swiped at the tears lingering on her cheeks, acknowledging the words that had haunted her all night long. The same words she'd whispered to a sleeping Ryan in a tight, aching voice just before she'd slipped from his bed in the early-morning hours before dawn.

Not only had she snuck out on him, but she'd left the key to his house on the nightstand, along with a hastily written note that she'd see him tonight at the party. Her manner of leaving said what she couldn't put into words—she was ending their affair. After the New Year's Eve party they'd revert to the friendly acquaintances they'd been before.

He wasn't going to be happy to find her gone, or with the cowardly way in which she'd executed her departure—a move born of pure self-preservation, because in that moment when he'd declared his love, she'd finally accepted that she'd fallen for Ryan Matthews deeper than she'd ever intended. And although it was too late to protect her emotions, she could still safeguard what was left of her heart, which hurt as it had never hurt before.

She swallowed back another well of tears and rubbed her hand along the chair's armrest. Without a doubt, she'd wanted Ryan. She'd wanted last night with every fiber of her being. So she'd selfishly taken from him when she'd *known* she couldn't give back—because openly loving him, trusting him with her future, was a heartbreaking combination. It was a harsh lesson taught to her by her father and backed up by her short-lived relationship with Lane. And with Ryan's career being his foremost priority, along with his profession contradicting her need for stability and security, she couldn't depend on him to be there in the long run. By his own admittance, long-term relationships weren't his forte, and she wasn't willing to be the casualty of a failed experiment.

So, she was cutting her losses, letting him go, and taking with her all the glorious, wondrous memories he'd given her. It didn't compare to the real feel of being held in his arms, hearing his deep laughter, or seeing the sexy gleam in his eyes as he attempted to seduce her with one of his erotic shenanigans. She'd never be able to look at a cake without remembering his *slippery, sensual, erotic* promise, which he'd more than fulfilled last night. And taking a bath would be an excruciating reminder of how much fun and pleasure he'd shown her when a couple shared the experience.

She drew a deep, shuddering breath, knowing she'd

miss him, knowing she'd *never* regret what they'd shared.

A loud pounding on her door made her jump and jostled her back to the present. She'd known this confrontation was coming, and though she'd resigned herself to facing him, she just hadn't expected the encounter to be at six o'clock in the morning.

"Dammit, Jessica," he said, his deep, gruff voice muffled through the door separating them. "I know you're in there so open up. I'm not leaving until we talk."

She wouldn't expect him to. He wasn't a coward as she'd been. Ryan wanted answers, an explanation, and since he'd been nothing but sincere with her, he deserved her honesty in return. And maybe, if she was lucky, once their discussion was over he'd understand her position and they'd be able to part as friends.

He pounded on the door again, making the whole apartment seem to shake with the wrath that stood out in the hallway. Before he could wake her neighbors, she unlocked and opened her door, feeling surprisingly calm after having had two hours to purge herself of her tears and misery.

He brushed past her into the living room, then stopped, jammed his hands on his hips, and *glared* at her. Not only was he not happy, he was *furious*.

Judging by his appearance, she guessed he'd woken up, realized she was gone, and had grabbed the first article of clothing he'd come into contact with, which was the shirt and slacks he'd worn last night, now wrinkled from being tossed haphazardly to the floor. He'd been in such a hurry that he hadn't bothered to tuck in the tails, nor had he put on any socks. His dark hair was still tousled from her running her fingers through the strands last night, his unshaven jaw was clenched, and his eyes were dark, but rimmed in a bright shade of gold that seared her straight to her soul.

Praying that he wouldn't hate her for what she had to do, for what she'd done, she closed the door, leaned against it, and waited for him to unleash the anger raging just below the surface.

The tempest didn't take long to erupt. He swept a hand in the air, his expression thunderous, showing her a very different side to the sexy, teasing, tender man she knew. "What the hell was that all about, you sneaking out in the middle of the night like I was some kind of one-night stand?"

Even though she knew his question was born of anger, she inwardly winced at his tawdry reference, when last night—the whole month they'd spent together—had been anything but a cheap tryst. The time with him had been magical, sensual, unforgettable.

And temporary.

"I'm sorry," she whispered around the tight knot of emotion in her throat, belatedly realizing the apology was inadequate for her departure, which had been instigated by pure panic.

She drew a breath and flattened her palms against the cool door. "I thought me leaving would be the easiest way to…"

"End things between us?" he finished for her.

The man was very perceptive, but she'd discovered that characteristic about him the past month, among others. "Yes."

"You thought *wrong*, Jessica," he said, his tone vibrating with resentment, and a deeper layer of hurt. "I don't take what we did last night lightly, not after wanting you for the past year. When I went to bed with you, when we made *love*, I expected to wake up with you next to me. Instead, I find the key to my house, and a facsimile of a 'Dear John' letter on my nightstand.''

The pressure in her chest felt near unbearable, but she lifted her chin and clung to her convictions. "I know I didn't handle this morning the best way—"

"No, you didn't," he interrupted heatedly, and slowly stalked toward her, a ruthless light in his eyes. "And I don't appreciate you making decisions for me when I'm capable of making them for myself."

Her stomach clenched as he neared. She didn't fear *him*, just his arguments. He was a man used to debating, and winning, and this was one issue on which she had to stand firm. "I made the decision to leave, to end our affair, for myself *and* for you."

He stopped two feet away, the heat and energy radiating off him nearly palpable. "How...*considerate* of you. But what makes you believe I want us to end?"

There was the rub in their situation. Right now, he was so caught up in the physical aspect of their relationship, the new and fresh emotions of love, that he didn't want the euphoria to end. Neither did she, but she was a realist and knew better, and sustaining what was between them now into the distant future was another matter altogether. And too huge a risk to her heart.

Before she could formulate a response, his gaze narrowed and he continued in a demanding tone. "I want reasons, Jessica. Are you ending things because I'm a divorce attorney?"

His question wasn't unwarranted. From the first time she'd met him at Brooke's cabin a year ago she'd clung to that excuse to keep her attraction to him at bay. She'd been successful, until this month. During the course of the past four weeks, she'd discovered all her preconceived notions about him, about lawyers, had been a defense. She'd always felt the need to blame someone for destroying her family, and blaming her father, and his attorney, had been the easiest route.

There was so much more to Ryan than his profession, and that's what made her choice so difficult. She'd seen many facets to his personality, and beneath the charm and flirtatious manner was a good, kind, caring man. One who enjoyed his family and friends, but ultimately loved his job.

She shook her head in answer to his question, and tried to explain. "No, it's not because you're a divorce attorney, but your career, your ambition and drive, don't leave much room in your life for a committed relationship." The stable, secure kind of relationship she needed.

"How do you *know* that?"

The challenge was unmistakable, and she couldn't help but think of what a formidable opponent he'd be in the courtroom. "I've seen your dedication to your job. I know where you're heading in your firm, and what it's going to take to get there. Long hours. Personal sacrifices. Possibly no extra time to nurture a new relationship. Can you deny that?"

He stared at her for a long, hard moment, then exhaled a harsh breath. "No, I can't deny any of that, but I'm willing to find some kind of balance."

"Well, I can't risk that you might not be able to find that balance, that your goals won't mesh with what I need from a relationship, and that you'll decide after a few months or a year that it's so much easier and simpler remaining single and unattached. Which brings us back to ending our relationship now, before things get any more complicated."

"I love you, Jessica," he said, frustration and tenderness mingling in his voice. "That's about as complicated as it gets."

Her knees nearly buckled at the declaration, made in the light of morning. She didn't doubt his sincerity, not for one second, but the emotional blackmail was excruciating. "I know you do."

He shook his head in confusion. "Doesn't that mean anything to you?"

She couldn't answer him, because his love meant too much. Rejecting it was the most difficult thing she'd ever had to do.

A low, frustrated sound erupted from his chest, and he spun around and paced to the other side of the small living room. Then he abruptly stopped and turned back to face her. "I get it now," he said, a dawning realization touching his features. "You're leaving *me* before I can leave *you*, aren't you?"

Her heart thudded in her chest, and she moved away from the door, but kept her distance from Ryan. "I have no idea what you're talking about."

"Don't you?" A dark brow winged upward. "I'm talking about the fact that you're scared I'll leave you at some point in our relationship, so you're doing it first. It's easier for you not to invest your emotions and not to believe what I feel for you is real, than to trust that I won't hurt you."

She bristled defensively. "You can't make that kind of promise."

"Can anyone?" he countered. He waited a tension-filled minute for her to answer. Then he smiled grimly. "Judging by your silence, I'm taking it that you agree the answer is no. Which means that although you're afraid of being abandoned and alone, that's exactly where you'll stay, because no man will be able to make you that promise. The only guarantee I can give you is how I feel about you. The rest is up to you to trust me."

Despite loving him, she wasn't sure she had the strength and emotional fortitude to put her faith in his hands. Doubts and uncertainties overwhelmed her, tugging her in two different directions. Hot, scalding tears burned her eyes, and she valiantly blinked them back. She pressed her fingers to her trembling lips and turned away so he wouldn't witness her insecurities, even though he knew every single one of them.

A long moment passed, and she flinched when she heard the front door open then close behind Ryan, leaving her completely and utterly alone. The quiet and solitude wrapping around her was absolute, more so than it had ever been.

HE'D DONE ALL HE COULD. Ryan knew that, but it didn't stop him from replaying his conversation with Jessica over and over in his mind, scrutinizing the rebuttals he'd issued to her arguments, trying to figure out what he could have said to sway her, to make her realize his intentions were pure.

There was nothing else he could do. The realization was tough to swallow. For the first time in his life he felt utterly defeated, not over a case, but a woman. A very special, beautiful, sassy, stubborn woman. He'd given Jessica factual evidence of his devotion, not only in words, but in actions, and none of his efforts had made a difference.

Unable to concentrate on the speech he needed to write for tonight's surprise party for Brooke and Marc, he set his pen aside and scrubbed both hands down his face. The knot in his chest hadn't abated since he'd walked out of Jessica's apartment, and he doubted he'd find relief any time soon. Especially not tonight, when he'd be so close to Jessica, but unable to touch her, tease her, and revel in the fact that she was exclusively his.

He'd never intended to fall in love with her, but she'd shown him what was missing from his life...love, laughter, and shared intimacies with one very special person. True, he'd managed to remain uncommitted since he was eighteen, but he was coming to believe that being a bachelor hadn't been a conscious choice as much as not finding the right person to complement him.

Jessica complemented him, physically, emotionally, and intellectually, in a way that made her feel like his other half. His soul mate. A piece of himself that he hadn't known was missing until she'd entered his life. And deep inside, beneath layers of doubts and uncertainties instilled by a negligent father and an unstable childhood, he suspected that she felt the same.

With a weary sigh, he sat back in his chair and rolled the pen between his fingers. Despite his earlier debate with Jessica, he knew he couldn't force her into believing he'd never deliberately hurt her, or walk out on her without a backward glance. She had to realize his sincerity came straight from his heart, driven by an emotion that was turning out to be more painful than joyful.

After another half hour of brooding over his situation, Ryan resigned himself to the inevitable. There was nothing else he could do to convince Jessica of his love, except let her go. There was nothing else left to say...except goodbye.

And with that aching thought filling his head, he put pen to paper and wrote the toast to Brooke and Marc, using the speech as a way to congratulate the happy couple, put his own feelings down on paper, and issue a final farewell to Jessica.

11

"*SURPRISE!*" a loud assembly of guests chorused as
Brooke and Marc walked into Ryan's house right on
schedule a half hour after everyone else had arrived.

Standing at the front of the group in the silky blue
dress she'd bought for the occasion, Jessica watched as
Brooke gasped and pressed a hand to her chest, her
eyes wide with confusion. Beside her sister, Marc
looked on with bemusement as he helped Brooke take
off her coat, seemingly unsure of what he and his wife
had just stepped into.

Brooke's gaze found Jessica in the gathering of
friends and family crowded in Ryan's foyer. "What's
all this about?" she asked, bewilderment coloring her
voice. Her fingers fluttered self-consciously down the
front of her slim black dress, smoothing out imaginary
wrinkles. "I thought this was a New Year's Eve party."

Ryan stepped forward before Jessica could respond,
and her heart twisted painfully in her chest, adding to
the constant ache she'd experienced since arriving two
hours ago to help him with the last-minute preparations for the party. Despite what had transpired between them last night, and this morning, he'd been polite and cordial, almost indifferent, and whenever
possible he'd kept his distance. He acted as if they'd
never spent the past month getting to know each other.
As if they'd never indulged in sensual fantasies and

made love last night. As if he'd never told her he loved her.

And even though Jessica acknowledged that it had been her choice to end their affair, that she'd been the one to drive him to such extreme measures, the distance he'd already established between them added to her misery. If she was fortunate, in another twenty years the memories they'd created together would no longer smother her. And she'd be able to say his name without feeling as though a piece of her soul had been ripped from her. And maybe, just maybe, she'd be able to live through a whole minute without being consumed by thoughts of him.

"It *is* a New Year's Eve party," Ryan confirmed with an easy grin. He shook Marc's hand in greeting, then placed a chaste kiss on Brooke's cheek. "But it's also a surprise party for you and Marc since you had a small wedding and no reception."

Sentimental emotions touched Brooke's features, and she once again sought Jessica. "Did you know about this, Jess?"

She nodded, her throat too tight to speak.

"Actually, it was her idea," Ryan said, slipping his hands into the front pockets of his black trousers that complemented his black-and-beige pinstriped shirt. "I just supplied the house for the party."

He'd done more than that, and they both knew it. He'd been responsible for a good many of the decisions that had gone into the planning, from the decorations, to the menu, to the huge gift basket overflowing with sensual items, which was sitting on one of the tables laden with presents from the other guests.

"Well, you two shouldn't have," Marc said, though it was obvious he appreciated the gesture, as well.

Jessica forced a cheerful smile. "I wanted to do something special for the both of you." She enveloped each of them in a warm hug, then grabbed her sister's hand and tugged her toward the waiting guests. "Now come on in, and enjoy your evening."

Now that the guests of honor had arrived, the party atmosphere turned lively, loud, and fun. Laughter and conversation filtered through the house, the buffet enticed people to eat, and Jessica did her best to have a good time and keep her gaze off Ryan. Yet out of sight was not out of her mind. And every time she thought about not seeing him after tonight, she felt herself die a little more inside.

A few hours later, everyone gathered in the living room to watch Brooke and Marc open their gifts. They received everything from kitchen appliances, to basic accessories, and other practical items. The sensual bathroom products she and Ryan had selected were a hit, and caused a bit of ribald teasing. While Marc fended off good-natured ribbing from the male guests, Jessica glanced across the room where she knew Ryan was standing, with his shoulder braced against the wall and a drink in hand.

Her breath caught when she found him watching her, a flicker of warmth in his eyes, as if he, too, was remembering the fun they'd had testing their own supply of those items. She recalled how incredibly patient he'd been with her...and she'd repaid him by rejecting his love.

He looked away when his sister, Natalie, came up to his side and said something to him. Ignoring the sense of loss settling over her, Jessica returned her attention to her sister and Marc, and was chagrined to realize that Brooke had caught the exchange between her and

Ryan. Her sister's brow quirked curiously at her, and Jessica pretended not to understand the questioning look.

Once the gift opening was over, Jessica mingled with the guests, then met up with her sister, who was enjoying a slice of one of the cakes. Brooke took a bite of the confection and rolled her eyes heavenward as she savored the taste.

"Oh, wow, this cake is *incredible*," Brooke said, and held out a forkful to Jessica. "Do you want a bite?"

The dessert Brooke offered was the Better Than Sex Cake. Jessica suppressed a shiver of recollection and shook her head. She'd be so grateful when the evening was over and she could escape everything that reminded her of Ryan and the time they'd spent together.

She'd return to her quiet, lonely apartment and continue her quiet, lonely, solitary life, a little voice in the back of her mind taunted. Before she could stop herself, a painful sigh unraveled out of her.

Brooke tipped her head, regarding her with concern. "Hey, are you okay?"

"Sure. I'm great." Her voice vibrated with false lightness, and she added a quick smile as backup. "Why?"

"You just seem, well, upset about something." Brooke took another bite of the dessert, and seemed to contemplate Jessica's mood. "Did you and Ryan have an argument?"

Oh, yeah, a huge, life-altering one.

"I mean, you must have had to spend some time together while planning this surprise party," Brooke went on while finishing her cake. "And I know how the two of you are around each other. The air fairly crackles with tension when you're together. But now it seems like you're avoiding each other."

"Don't we always?" she quipped.

"Not like this, Jess. You're *deliberately* avoiding each other, and despite your lawyer jokes and Ryan's teasing, that's never kept the two of you *apart* when you're in the same room." She set her plate aside. "Is something going on between the two of you?"

She wanted so badly to confide in her sister, but her emotions were in such turmoil, she didn't know where to begin, or what to say.

And then she lost the opportunity as the *ping, ping, ping* of silver against crystal captured everyone's attention. The guests grew quiet, and all eyes turned to Ryan, who stood in the middle of the living room with a glass of champagne in his hand.

He smiled, but his eyes lacked their normal sparkle. "It's ten minutes to midnight, and before we bring in the new year, I'd like for everyone to grab a drink so I can make a toast to Marc and Brooke."

It took nearly five minutes for family and friends to grab their choice of drink and settle back into the room. Once everyone was present, and Marc and Brooke were situated next to Ryan to receive his best-man speech, he cleared his throat and began.

"I've known Marc for quite a few years now, and I always thought he'd remain a bachelor forever, or at least that was his plan." Chuckles rippled through the small audience before Ryan continued. "When Marc fell in love with Brooke, I knew that she had to be a really special woman, one with a giving heart and the capacity to accept Marc for who and what he was. I knew she'd be the kind of woman who'd be his best friend through trials and triumphs. It is said that no man is complete until he finds the right woman to marry, and it's clear that Brooke has made Marc's life complete. Every man should be so fortunate."

Jessica stood behind Brooke and Marc, and belatedly realized her mistake in positioning herself so close to the bride and groom when Ryan's gaze subtly shifted to her. A frisson of awareness shot through her, and her insides began to tremble.

He didn't look away, and she couldn't either. "I've only been in love once, but I understand how powerful that emotion can be. I also know that there are times when love can be painful and trying, so I'd like to say a few things for you to keep in mind for the years ahead. Love without fear. Trust without questioning. Accept without change, and desire each other without inhibitions. Always believe in one another, and always have faith." He raised his flute of champagne to the happy couple, and everyone followed his lead. "Here's to love and laughter, and your happily ever after."

"Hear, hear," the guests echoed jovially, and Jessica was hardly aware of someone next to her clinking their glass against hers as she watched Marc kiss her sister with the kind of the love and tenderness Ryan had shown her.

Emotions clamored in her chest, her mind spun, and she struggled to keep herself grounded. Tears tightened her throat and burned the back of her eyes. Though Ryan's toast was for Brooke and Marc, the profound words beckoned to her, and made her realize what she'd never, ever have in her life—love, laughter, and her own happily ever after.

"Hey, everybody," someone in the room called out. "It's the countdown to midnight!"

The guests began counting down from ten, until finally the old year rolled into the new one and everyone cheered, hugged, and wished one another a happy new year.

Unable to participate in the ritual when she had absolutely nothing to celebrate, Jessica slipped from the room as inconspicuously as possible, taking her heartache with her.

BROOKE FOUND HER in the downstairs study minutes later. Jessica barely had time to swipe the tears from her cheeks before her sister laid into her.

"I *knew* something was going on between you and Ryan. He might have made that toast to Marc and me, but he was looking at *you*, Jessica." Brooke crossed her arms over her chest, exerting her big-sister presence. "Out with it," she demanded.

Jessica didn't bother to pretend she didn't know what Brooke was referring to. This time, she let the floodgates open and told her sister about the past month with Ryan, how she'd seen such a different side to him than she'd always believed, how she'd fallen in love with him, and ultimately, how she doubted her ability to trust in him because of her fears.

Brooke grabbed her hands and gave them a gentle squeeze. "Ah, Jess, sometimes following your heart is one of the most difficult things you'll ever do."

"But what if—"

Brooke shook her head, cutting off her sister's argument. "There are no 'what ifs' when you're in love. It just *is*. And despite what you might believe, not every man is like Dad."

"You know," she breathed, not at all surprised that her sister understood her so well.

"Yeah, I know that his leaving devastated you and

made you feel insecure about so many things. I know our life was tough, but we made it just fine, Jess." Brooke smiled, and brushed a stray strand of hair off her cheek. "*You* made it just fine. And I don't want to see you lose the best thing that has ever come into your life because you're afraid of trusting your true instincts."

She moved away from her sister and glanced at the hardbound books tucked in an oak bookshelf, unable to relinquish deeper insecurities. "What if I want more from Ryan than he can give me?"

"How do you know what he's capable of giving unless you give him a chance?" she countered.

And that meant trusting Ryan to put her first, and on those occasions when he couldn't because of the demands of his career, trusting herself to be strong enough to believe he'd always be there for her. To have faith that he'd find that balance.

"I don't think you'll ever forgive Dad for what he did to the family," Brooke said softly from behind her. "But don't let him sabotage your chance to be happy and possibly have a family of your own."

With that, her sister left the room to return to the party, leaving Jessica to contemplate her past, the present, and the future. And as she let go of bitter, resentful memories, she discovered a fortitude she never realized she possessed. A strength born of love. And the courage to grasp the kind of happiness Brooke had found for herself.

The kind of happiness Jessica had denied herself for far too long.

It seemed like forever before everyone cleared out of Ryan's house and she was alone with him. She was exhausted, but determined to speak with him. And she was nervous. Oh, Lord, especially that. So much was at stake. So much was at risk. Her heart. Her body. Her soul.

The rest of her life.

He frowned when he saw her standing in the entry-way all by herself, clearly not happy to find her still around. "What are you still doing here?" he asked, his tone flat and emotionless. "I thought you left when Brooke did."

"No, I only walked them out." Feeling her tenacity slip a serious notch, she blurted out her request before she lost her nerve. "Ryan...I'd like to talk to you."

He stared at her for a long, hard moment. "After this morning, I don't think there's anything left to say."

His reply startled her, rattling her composure and the carefully thought-out discussion she'd had planned. An awful sense of foreboding closed in on her like a vise around her chest. "What about..." *Us*. She nearly wept as the one word got tangled around those damnable insecurities of hers.

He jammed his hands on his hips, his expression impatient. "What about what?" he prompted gruffly.

She couldn't think straight. She needed time, time to gather her thoughts again. Her gaze swept the area, and she grasped the first excuse that came to mind. "What about the mess?"

Her offer to help only seemed to aggravate him more. "I have a cleaning crew coming in the morning, so go on home and don't worry about it." He paused for a moment, then said in a low, rough tone filled with too much emotion, "Goodbye, Jessica." With that, he turned and headed toward the kitchen.

She watched him go, her heart aching so fiercely she

could hardly breathe. He didn't want her anymore. And she had no one to blame except herself.

All because she hadn't been able to bring herself to trust in Ryan and his love.

RYAN HEARD THE FRONT DOOR open and close, and felt the finality of Jessica leaving right to the very depths of his soul. Bracing his hands on the kitchen counter, he squeezed his tired eyes shut and berated himself for being such an ass. The least he could have done was walk her to her car, but he hadn't been able to perform that simple gentlemanly task. It just hurt too damn much to be around her, and he hadn't wanted to stretch out their final goodbye.

All night he'd suffered with her being in his constant line of vision, of being wrapped in her scent when she happened to pass him. He'd tormented himself with private fantasies that included stripping off that sexy, silky blue dress she'd worn, fantasies of having her in his bed, his life.

And there, for a moment, he'd thought, hoped, that her reasons for wanting to stay behind had to do with them...not the mess.

Yeah, he was a mess all right, he thought with a disgusted snort. And he had no idea how he was going to get over loving and losing Jessica. One day at a time, he supposed.

A half an hour later, dead tired and weary to the bone, he locked up the house, turned off the lights, then dragged himself upstairs. By the time he'd reached his bedroom he had his shirt unbuttoned. Shrugging out of the garment, he tossed it over the end of his bed. He toed off his shoes, pulled off his socks and replaced his dress pants with a pair of sweat shorts.

He went to retrieve a T-shirt from his dresser, and that's when he caught sight of the pool of shimmering blue silk on the carpeted floor. His pulse raced as he followed a trail of silky stockings, a lacy black bra, and panties that led to the bathroom door, which had been left open a crack.

He pushed slowly against the door, and was greeted by the lush scent of strawberries, the flickering illumination of candlelight, and a woman lounging in his bathtub with a froth of bubbles coating the surface of the water. His gut clenched, with anxiety, and a hope so excruciating it nearly stole his breath.

Somehow, some way, he found his voice. "What are you doing here?"

Big blue eyes met his, and a tremulous smile touched her lips. "I'm attempting to prove a point."

Not sure where her scene for seduction was leading, he frowned down at her. "Excuse me?"

She drew a deep breath, and he watched in too much fascination as the bubbles quivered around the soft rise of her breasts. "You've shown me many times in the past month that actions speak louder than words. And since I was having trouble speaking downstairs, I thought I'd give *your* tactic a try to get your attention."

"You definitely have that." He rubbed a hand along the back of his neck, unable to relax the tense muscles bunching across his shoulders. "I thought you left."

"I never left, Ryan," she said, her voice as soft as the shadows in the bathroom. And just as vulnerable. "When it came right down to walking out your door, I couldn't do it. And I'm not going to leave until we talk."

Remembering how his bruised pride had prompted him to tell her they had nothing left to say to each other, this time he couldn't refuse her, not after she'd found the fortitude within herself to stay.

"All right," he conceded, and settled himself on the ledge of the tub. "Since you know exactly what I want from you, exactly how I feel about you, the floor is yours."

"I do want you, Ryan Matthews. More than I've ever wanted anyone in my life, and in ways that scare me."

"And what are you afraid of?" He knew her fears, but he had to know she'd resolved them for herself.

"I'm afraid of trusting a man for my happiness. Scared of giving in to the things I feel for you, and ending up being alone anyway." Her hands fluttered over the surface of the water, making it ripple enticingly. Making him wonder if she was completely naked beneath. "It's been very difficult for me, but I've come to realize that my expectations of you were unrealistic, and were just a way for me to maintain an emotional distance. As much as I wanted to when I first met you, I can't condemn you for being a divorce attorney, because you've shown me how kind, caring and fair you are, and that you'd never deliberately hurt someone for your own selfish gains. I have to believe what you do for a living, you do because you truly want to help people, because there is nothing egotistical or self-absorbed about you."

As much as her revelation pleased him, he remained quiet, needing more from her than that acceptance.

She seemed to sense that, too. "I know I can never forget what my father did to our family, the pain he put us through by abandoning us so completely, but

I'm ready to put that resentment behind me, because I can't bear the thought of losing you."

"And what about my career?" he asked, knowing her insecurities extended to that, too. "Are you able to accept the long hours ahead, the late nights, and the balance between my work and our relationship?"

"I'm willing to try," she replied honestly. "Knowing you love me makes a big difference, because I know you don't take something like that lightly."

His gaze held hers steadily. "No, I don't."

She bit her bottom lip, and reached out and touched a wet hand to his cheek. "You make me feel safe, and secure, and protected," she whispered in an aching voice. "And it's been so long since I've felt that way."

"I'll be here for you, Jessie." Gently capturing her wrist, he pressed a kiss in the center of her damp palm. "All you have to do is trust me, and believe in me."

"Oh, I do." The candlelight flickered, illuminating the beauty of her face, the vulnerability still lingering in her eyes. "And that's part of what frightens me so much. The depth of my feelings for you is very over-whelming, and like nothing I've ever experienced."

"And what do you feel?" The question prompted her to take that final leap of faith, to risk all.

She did. "I feel a richness and contentment I never knew was possible until you came into my life. I'm ready to trust my instincts, and I'm ready to trust my heart." She paused for a moment, then seemingly drew on that well of strength and confidence he always knew she possessed. "I'm naked beneath these bub-bles, Ryan. Physically and emotionally. I didn't want anything between us when I told you that I loved you so you'd know that I'm not hiding behind anything, that what I feel for you comes straight from my heart and soul."

He let go of her hand, briefly severing the connection between them, knowing when they came together again the bond would be stronger than before. "Stand up and show me."

A sensual dare. A provocative challenge. A final dissolving of those barriers that had kept her from being completely his.

Without an ounce of modesty, she stood, baring herself to him. His mouth went dry as he watched the slick water sluice down her naked body. Her skin glowed from the candlelight, and bubbles clung to her breasts, her belly, her thighs. He grew hard with a wanting and hunger he knew would never abate. Not in this lifetime.

She slipped her fingers beneath his chin and raised his gaze back to hers. "I love you, Ryan Matthews," she said, her clear voice and velvet blue eyes filled with the sentiment she spoke of.

His chest tightened, seeming to spill over with emotions for this woman who'd filled his life to overflowing. Straightening, he stripped off his shorts, not wanting her to be the only one naked—physically and emotionally. "I love *you*, Jessica Newman," he returned.

A sultry smile curved her mouth as she took a moment to appreciate the length of his body, and his obvious need for her. Passion and tenderness brightened her eyes when she met his gaze again.

"I love you without fear," she said, reciting the toast he'd written and had meant, on some level, for her. "I trust you without question. I accept you without change, and I desire you without inhibitions."

He stepped into the tub, but didn't touch her. "Will you always believe in me, and always have faith?"

"Yes," she breathed.

It was all he needed to hear. He sank into the warm, silky water, braced his back against the side, and pulled her with him so she straddled his hips. She gasped as his erection slid against the heat of her, and for as much as he ached to complete their union, he held back.

He smoothed damp, unruly strands away from her face. "Then I promise to give you love and laughter, and a happily ever after."

She stiffened, her eyes widening in shock. "Are you..."

"Proposing?" he suggested.

She settled her hands on his shoulders and nodded, hope and uncertainties mingling in her gaze.

He lazily, leisurely stroked his hands along her spine to her hips, loving the feel of her. "Yes, I am."

"You really want to marry me?" Disbelief tinged her voice. "I mean, that's a big step, a huge commitment—"

"One I'm finally ready for," he assured her. But doubts still lingered for her—he could see them in her expression, and suspected those uncertainties tied in to his profession. "Would you believe that working on divorce cases makes me more aware of how difficult it is to make a relationship work? I've felt that way for years, and I've developed an appreciation and respect for my parents' strong marriage. Those traditional values are what I want for myself. With you. And just so you know going into this, I want kids, too." He grinned, knowing that wouldn't be a problem for her at all. Knowing, too, how much fun they'd have making those babies.

A joyful moisture filled her eyes. "A family," she whispered.

"Yeah, a family," he agreed. "One for us to love, and share, and grow old with."

She wrapped her arms around his neck and held him close. "It scares me how much I need you, Ryan," she said after a poignant moment had passed.

Her open honesty humbled him. Tangling his fingers in her hair, he gently pulled her back, just enough to look into her eyes. The water lapped between them erotically, her taut nipples brushed against his chest, but Ryan resisted the urge to give in to the tantalizing delights beckoning to them. *Soon.*

"Hell, Jessie, this is all new to me, too." He smiled in understanding. "I was hoping we could figure out this love and forever thing together."

A shiver passed through her body, and a hint of remorse creased her delicate brows. "You're right, of course. We'll work on it together. I guess old insecurities die hard. Can you forgive me?"

"Ah, sweetheart, there's absolutely nothing to forgive." He caressed a thumb along her frown, making it disappear beneath his touch. "Just say you'll marry me so I'll know you'll always be mine."

A sassy, naughty sparkle suddenly entered her gaze. Sliding intimately closer, she squeezed her knees shamelessly against his hips. "Umm, do you think you could *coerce* me into saying yes?"

He groaned as his erection strained between them. Knowing her innocent request would lead to a thrilling build-up to her ultimate surrender, he played along.

"I'll certainly do my best," he drawled, and guided her warm and willing mouth to his.

Her lips parted, soft and welcoming. His tongue dipped and parried and swirled with hers in a slow, deep, rapacious kiss. Beneath the water, he glided his flattened palms up her thighs, until his thumbs parted her slick flesh, stroked rhythmically, and expertly brought her to that exquisite crest.

Stopping his illicit caresses before she fell over the edge, he lifted his head and met her heavy-lidded gaze. "Marry me," he murmured.

Her face was beautifully flushed with arousal and the heat of the water, her breathing heavy. "Maybe," she said huskily, then dampened her lips with her tongue. "I think you need to be more persuasive."

He grinned wickedly, and slanted his mouth possessively over hers. With his hands on her hips, he lifted her, brought her flush against his length, then let her sleek, wet body slowly glide back down his chest, his belly, until his hard, aroused flesh demanded entrance between her silky thighs. She moaned and shuddered, and with excruciating slowness, he impaled her on his shaft, sheathing himself in measured, gradual degrees until he was deep inside her.

He inhaled sharply as she rocked urgently against him, intending to coax him to a quick climax. He stilled her seductive movements with his hands on her waist and struggled for a semblance of control.

"Before I let you take advantage of me like you intend to, I need an answer first," he rasped, trying not to lose himself in the dark desire shimmering in her eyes. The pure adoration. "Be my wife, Jessie. My lover. My best friend."

Framing his face between her hands, she captured

his gaze in the romantic candlelight. "Yes," she said without hesitation. "I'll be all those things for you... your wife, your lover, your best friend."

A cocksure grin tipped his mouth. "It's nice to know I haven't lost my touch."

She rolled her eyes at his teasing comment. "Considering all the years ahead of us, I'll make sure you have plenty of practice."

Oh, he didn't doubt her claim for a second. And as he seduced her body with pleasure, and she gave of herself with abandon, he knew he was a lucky man, indeed.

Pamela Burford presents

The Wedding Ring

*Four high school friends and a pact—
every girl gets her ideal mate by thirty or be
prepared for matchmaking! The rules are
simple. Give your "chosen" man three
months...and see what happens!*

Love's Funny That Way
Temptation #812—on sale December 2000
It's no joke when Raven Muldoon falls in love with comedy
club owner Hunter—*brother* of her "intended."

I Do, But Here's the Catch
Temptation #816—on sale January 2001
Charli Ross is more than willing to give up her status as
last of a dying breed—the thirty-year-old virgin—to Grant.
But all *he* wants is marriage.

One Eager Bride To Go
Temptation #820—on sale February 2001
Sunny Bleecker is still waiting tables at Wafflemania when
Kirk comes home from California and wants to marry her.
It's as if all her dreams have finally come true—except...

Fiancé for Hire
Temptation #824—on sale March 2001
No way is Amanda Coppersmith going to let
The Wedding Ring rope her into marriage. But no matter
how clever she is, Nick is one step ahead of her...

*"Pamela Burford creates the
memorable characters readers love!"
—The Literary Times*

Visit us at www.eHarlequin.com   HTRING

It's hot...and it's out of control.

BLAZE

This winter is going to be hot, hot, hot!
Don't miss these bold, provocative,
ultra-sexy books!

SEDUCED by Janelle Denison
December 2000

Lawyer Ryan Matthews wanted sexy Jessica Newman the
moment he saw her. And she seemed to want him, too, but
something was holding her back. So Ryan decides it's time
to launch a sensual assault. He *is* going to have Jessica in
his bed—and he isn't above tempting her with her own
forbidden fantasies to do it....

SIMPLY SENSUAL by Carly Phillips
January 2001

When P.I. Ben Callahan agrees to take the job of watching
over spoiled heiress Grace Montgomery, he figures it's easy
money. That is, until he discovers gorgeous Grace has a
reckless streak a mile wide and is a serious threat to his
libido—and his heart. Ben isn't worried about keeping
Grace safe. But can he protect her from his loving lies?

Don't miss this daring duo!

HARLEQUIN®
Temptation.

Visit us at www.eHarlequin.com   HTBLAZEW

Tyler Brides

It happened one weekend...

Quinn and Molly Spencer are delighted to accept three bookings for their newly opened B&B, Breakfast Inn Bed, located in America's favorite hometown, Tyler, Wisconsin.

But Gina Santori is anything but thrilled to discover her best friend has tricked her into sharing a room with the man who broke her heart eight years ago....

And Delia Mayhew can hardly believe that she's gotten herself locked in the Breakfast Inn Bed basement with the sexiest man in America.

Then there's Rebecca Salter. She's turned up at the Inn in her wedding gown. Minus her groom.

Come home to Tyler for three delightful novellas by three of your favorite authors: Kristine Rolofson, Heather MacAllister and Jacqueline Diamond.

HARLEQUIN®
Makes any time special ™

Visit us at www.eHarlequin.com

PHTB

◈ **HARLEQUIN**®

makes any time special—online...

eHARLEQUIN.com

your romantic escapes

—Indulgences—
♥ Monthly guides to indulging yourself, such as:
   ★ Tub Time: A guide for bathing beauties
   ★ Magic Massages: A treat for tired feet

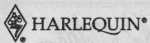

—Horoscopes—
♥ Find your daily Passionscope, weekly Lovescopes and Erotiscopes

♥ Try our compatibility game

—Reel Love—
♥ Read all the latest romantic movie reviews

—Royal Romance—
♥ Get the latest scoop on your favorite royal romances

—Romantic Travel—
♥ For the most romantic destinations, hotels and travel activities

HINTE1

If you enjoyed what you just read,
then we've got an offer you can't resist!

Take 2 bestselling
love stories FREE!
Plus get a FREE surprise gift!

Clip this page and mail it to Harlequin Reader Service®

IN U.S.A.
3010 Walden Ave.
P.O. Box 1867
Buffalo, N.Y. 14240-1867

IN CANADA
P.O. Box 609
Fort Erie, Ontario
L2A 5X3

YES! Please send me 2 free Harlequin Temptation® novels and my free surprise gift. Then send me 4 brand-new novels every month, which I will receive before they're available in stores. In the U.S.A., bill me at the bargain price of $3.34 plus 25¢ delivery per book and applicable sales tax, if any*. In Canada, bill me at the bargain price of $3.80 plus 25¢ delivery per book and applicable taxes**. That's the complete price and a savings of 10% off the cover prices—what a great deal! I understand that accepting the 2 free books and gift places me under no obligation ever to buy any books. I can always return a shipment and cancel at any time. Even if I never buy another book from Harlequin, the 2 free books and gift are mine to keep forever. So why not take us up on our invitation. You'll be glad you did!

142 HEN C22U
342 HEN C22V

Name	(PLEASE PRINT)	
Address	Apt.#	
City	State/Prov.	Zip/Postal Code

* Terms and prices subject to change without notice. Sales tax applicable in N.Y.
** Canadian residents will be charged applicable provincial taxes and GST.
   All orders subject to approval. Offer limited to one per household.
   ® are registered trademarks of Harlequin Enterprises Limited.

TEMP00   ©1998 Harlequin Enterprises Limited

CELEBRATE VALENTINE'S DAY WITH HARLEQUIN®'S LATEST TITLE—

Stolen Memories

Available in trade-size format, this collector's edition contains three full-length novels by *New York Times* bestselling authors Jayne Ann Krentz and Tess Gerritsen, along with national bestselling author Stella Cameron.

TEST OF TIME by **Jayne Ann Krentz**—
He married for the best reason.... She married for the only reason.... Did they stand a chance at making the only reason the real reason to share a lifetime?

THIEF OF HEARTS by **Tess Gerritsen**—
Their distrust of each other was only as strong as their desire. And Jordan began to fear that Diana was more than just a thief of hearts.

MOONTIDE by **Stella Cameron**—
For Andrew, Greer's return is a miracle. It had broken his heart to let her go. Now fate has brought them back together. And he won't lose her again...

Make this Valentine's Day one to remember!

Look for this exciting collector's edition on sale January 2001 at your favorite retail outlet.

HARLEQUIN®
Makes any time special ™

Visit us at www.eHarlequin.com

PHSM